`

Blind Extortion

1 Smokers grant
2 Taking off
3 The ugly mob
4 Harbourside hookers
5 In the proverbial
6 Its getting better man !
7 Beats
8 The buffer
9 Blind extortion
10 The Fly
11 Jonny Mathis

Dialogue.

Min - man
Nae - no
Fit - what
Ken - know
Aye - yes
The morn - tomorrow
Oot - out
Cannae - can't
Bar - 9 ounces
Gonnae - going to
Aboot - about
Hame - home
Doon - down
Toon -town

CHAPTER ONE

I awoke excitedly at the prospects which

lay ahead in my day at college in the granite city , for today wasn't just any day , today was the day us students savour for today was student loan day . Allow me to put this into prospective for you , hundreds of students barely out of school or at best under twenty have been used to their pot washing wages for two nights a week work , when suddenly they receive fifteen hundred pounds in their banks or in cheque on the same day .

   The majority go to cash converters , buy some dodgy converse boots and chords and revel in their new found fortune down the union with pints of tennent's and shady chat up lines ,

 I have always been a bit of a dreamer and tried in vain to put my early entrepreneur skills to maximum use with many failed and successful businesses. I had a finger board business at school in 1991 making mini skate boards with Perspex and old toy car wheels and designing tracks all for free money if I made them myself , even in primary school my old man was called by the head teacher because I was selling conkers that I'd gathered off a big tree in England , they were bigger than the ones we got around here in this Scottish village and with that came the price of a pound each in my pocket . At the age of twelve on returning from a school trip in France by coach I was down to my my last 100 francs which was around a tenner back then. We stopped at Calais to go to the shops and stock up for our return through Britain , everyone else had plenty of cash for a twelve year old , I didn't . I knew I needed to invest my ten when I stumbled across crates of cola in cans , now this was

the middle of summer in france , 50 kids on a bus , it was sweltering stuck in that mobile greenhouse and my seat was next to the bus' fridge . These cans were 10p each so I bought 50 for a cool

fiver and got back to the bus to bypass the teachers funny looks and to get the fridge stocked up , within 3 hours I had sold the lot at 50p each , now I had 30 quid back of which ten went in the fruity and got me a fifty quid jackpot . I had doubled the money I originally had to spend in the first place and was going home in over a hundred percent profit . I was really proud and smug about my transactions .

So you can see the potential in my mind of 17-20 year olds with loads of cash , happy days

Now to get them to invest in me for mine and their good fortune . We all smoked weed or knew a lot of people who did , they collectively had money to give to me to get us the best deal on what we thought was bulk at the time . Seven others had agreed to pay me 500 pounds each a nine bar (9oz) of sputnik. I got 8 bars for 400 each which if you do the maths makes me 300 and a free bar to get my little business going while the others got their little sectors covered with their nine bars . My plan was for me to sell small deals to friends and colleagues and get the repeat business from the original investors to give me a healthy study allowance . I had arranged through some friends in the city to get a drop at my flat in the city centre , the deal was arranged that a bloke on a motorbike would come and provide the weed while I gave him the cash , this could be dodgy for us lot as we were vulnerable to a set up or robbery but it went well , I had matt , Scott and Wayne in the bedroom listening out and ready to pounce if anything went wrong and it

didn't. The bloke on the bike was called Archie and we exchanged numbers and that was that. After this I would have had the cash to get it from England where it is half the price and double the earning potential .

   Things are not that simple though at that age , which isn't an excuse , as I said I have always been a dreamer.

    At this time in my life I had just returned from London where I worked for the summer while staying at my old mans , my plan was always to return to the granite city as I always and always will feel like the place is my true home , I lived at my dads with my girlfriend of the time and on returning to Aberdeen we drifted apart , I had loads of catching up to do with my mates out in the country as she did with hers in the town , she promptly packed and it was the good old bachelor life for me . I let my mate Wayne move in as he was always in need of a bit of help and I was a sucker for helping lost causes , He would sit about all day waiting for me to come home and feed the bugger. I really didn't mind though as he was good company and would do anything for me and always backed me up , we met at school when I was 13 , he was from a place called glenrothes and they all talked a bit funny in comparison to us back then , he would say "wan" instead of "one" , "baws" instead of "balls" , he made friends with us popular lot at school straight away by hitting some one we didn't like or offering to spend his dinner money on ten 'lammie bammies' (lambert & butler) in return for

two fags in the morning , it was always a
bidding war in the playground to see who
could get the best deal out of him , Though
who ever gave him the cigs in the morning
had to put up with him in his stupid stupid
accent saying "go leaves us twos man" all
day long . He was six and a half foot tall
and
skinnier than an anorexic Ethiopian .
  My flat was only at most 6 metre square
and that included a bedroom , lounge ,
bathroom , bedroom and kitchen all
crammed in with all mod cons and white
goods , perfect for a 20 year old with his
mate Wayne ' streak of piss ' Hockeye
crashing on my super comfy 15 year old
recliner in the parlour
of my penthouse situated smack bang in
the middle of the wealthy Granite City .
We moonlighted as window cleaners for
some casino junkie from Troon who had less
brains than a blonde cavewoman and as
much ambition . He would spend our hard
earned ladder scaling cash on a Thursday
and then cower in his flat when we were

buzzing him on a Friday demanding our dosh .

This lasted a few weeks with us being gullible enough to be convinced we had to go and slog it out on a Monday morning on the North Sea coast just to get half our wages . One Monday after the ginger gambler dodged us all weekend I decided to screw him up back by planning to do with his workforce what he does with us . We gathered at our usual meeting place of my flat on the Monday morn , eagerly awaiting his buzz on the downstairs door with child like excitement and giddiness .

Sean arrived as we knew he would , he buzzed the door as usual and jumped in his car to wait , we were all rolling about laughing as we watched him angrily get back out of his car with his face the colour of his ginger hair and buzz three times longer and louder and looked up to the window .

I then pulled the curtains back so he knew we were there and quickly dropped them closed just too really really wind the ginger

gambler up . He stormed off , phoned me from home where me and wayne hung up our squeegee for good ,
and good old Wayne threw in an insult of "stay away from our hoose you wee ginge or I'll chin ye , ye bam " ,even though Wayne himself was a closet ginger or as he put it " its no ginger , its fucking strawberry blonde man " .

CHAPTER TWO

 The business was taking off as word spread that I was the man for weed from Banchory to Aberdeen and an area covering 10 miles radius , the custom at first was always People I knew either from school or from the village that I grew up in .

Archie phoned me up on the mobile one day when it was time to reorder for the Sunday coming .

" Alright min , how many
You needing the morn min?"

I stupidly got ahead of myself and reordered for my usual cash paying custom before rambling on to foolishly demonstrate my selling power ,

" I've definitely sold the 4 for cash but a couple of other lads have said they could shift some for us and then a couple of students can pay cash for two..."

Archie pleasantly interrupted in a dulcet stoned slow tone

" fit I'll do fae ye then is gie ye 8 aye , 4 cashers min the morn and then four laid on till next Sunday aye , ye'll shift ah that nae bother will ye , I'll drop it to ye the morns night ."

That was the start of what I was about to get involved in and a very full time unchosen profession . Without realising I had just got in to debt to the sum of nearly £2000 to people I didn't know , and for what I was going to find out in the future people that anybody really didn't want to know for their own sake . Though Archie was always the pleasant middle man overly eager to push on to you , what he was getting pushed on to him .

   Now that I had this unpaid for supply , I knew I needed trustworthy people to leave it with to get rid of on their terms , little franchises around the region .

   There was an older lad in Banchory in his thirties , Clarky , now I have known of and known for quite some time . He hung about with the skinheads in their thirties , the group that every village has , the group that rolls with the times and never really grows up , the group that wore knee length doc Martins at school , had Mohicans in the eighties and liked punk , then progressed to the ecstasy and warehouse parties of the early nineties ,d j Carl Cox , and then oakenfold , you get the picture . They are in their forties now with the odd kid and the weekend cocaine habit but their morals and values have remained the same just dampened down a bit in their mid life . Clarky was liked by all of this lot who were looked upto in our village but they didn't seem to want to have this acknowledged by too many people . After all this is a small village where nobodies business is ever really private and rumours circulated the village for 15 years about Clarky , every year getting worse and worse as to things he has really done . In a stupid moment as a kid he robbed a woman's bag , and never lived it down by the time he was 35 the story went that he marched her to a cash point after putting cigs out on her head , this was nonsense , he was really a pussy cat who seeked out praise from people and was always over pleased to do something for you and keep reminding you of his good deeds . He had a sixteen year old brother he still shared a room with and we called him mini Clarky , he idolised his big brother and copied his jeans and wore a smaller bomber jacket the same as his bros. Ideal set up then , some one who was over eager to please and his wee bro , 2 vastly different age groups who all bought what we were selling .

I started Clarky off on half a bar , laid on of course , so that he could then sell half scores and scores to people in the village , eighths and quarter ounces .

I had to stop selling the small amounts out in the village and seek out new punters for the smaller deals of quarters and ounces , otherwise I would be treading on my own toes and undercutting the people that I needed onside . Clarky did as I knew he would , he sold out in the allocated time period what he was given and ultimately paid for it . There was a drawback with him for which I was willing to ignore, he would call me every time he sold something , and half a bar in small deals is about 30 various deals . I did say he was eager to please and loved getting the praise . I could play up to this though when he would excitedly call me in a fast and slurry voice

" Alrite Santos , how's you? Things are flying down my end , just sold another score for 30 min , I will be needing more , maybe I can pay cash in a week or two if you keep things coming , know what I'm saying min"

 I had to but in just to get my pal even giddier .

 " Well oot clarky , nae bother , you can have as much as you like now , and I know I can trust you, you're my main man"

 He responded in his childish giddiness .

" Aye . Am I min , really ? Do I sell the most for you then . Aye . Cool cool , and I will do twice that for you Santos , want some cash ? " ,

 "chill oot Clarky , just give me it Sunday , or use it to buy a bar off me if things are going that well and you have the primetime weekend slot to shift it "

 "Aye aye , cool cool min , good thinking , but fit if I Cannae shift it all "

 "Clarky you have 3 days and you only need to get half a bars money with a bar to play with , it will put you right ahead and paying for cashers within a week"

I threw in a couple more compliments about him being my main man and he was swiftly off the phone to pursue more sales and collection to get his bar in time to shift it for Sunday .

That inevitably got me thinking , if he can do it then so can Others and there will be this whole lot of people from college and further a field that could do the same , I could offer the punters who pay cash for one bar , a second on a seven day tick , meaning that in the very near future all my punters will have enough spare cash and more to keep buying for cash , just as long as I pushed them for the money as so it would not be sitting around ready to be spent . Even taking what they had took in in a morning's work , just so they could transfer that eventually in to bars , purchased upfront for cash . It was a theory I thought where everyone would win . In theory it did work , at that time I was yet to see if the theory would turn into practise and work for us all .

  At this time around our town and further field I was seen to always have a wad of cash , a cocky swagger inherited from all the time I had previously spent in my original hometown of Manchester where you inherit the confident swagger of the Gallagher brothers , the don't give a fuck attitude of Ian brown , the quick wit of the great late Bernard manning and the capability to hold your booze and weed in the way that would make Shaun Ryder and bez proud . This inevitably got me interest from the fairer sex and not usually for the right reasons , you see up there in banchory most people have a good amount of capital and houses in one of Britain's most expensive regions due to the oil boom in Aberdeen in the seventies . These men moved from England to work in the oil business and made the little villages in to little towns and along the way picked up nice brides and had good looking kids who where approaching 20 at this time in my life and were very keen on boys like

their dad who could buy them nice things ,
eat in the best restaurants . I had always
managed to pull the stunners back then
and even though half the time I didn't like
the girl I was with . They just looked good
and the older lads in the town always
wondered how I did it . One girl came
along at this time who I had my eye on for
a while but I was seeing this other little
trophy missus , I soon enough ended it
when I got wind that Sian was keen on me ,
or effectively my wallet . Sian was a
daddy's girl but an absolute stunner and
spoilt with it , her dad didn't like me
because of my big brother Jay's recent
drug dealing past . I wasn't arsed , he
didn't have to know . The bonus with Sian
was that her old man bought her a car and
she loved football and driving so she would
pick me up from my flat in the city and take
me out to the village and give me lifts as I
didn't drive at this time . She
was very demanding though and would
myther for me to meet her at the dearest
Indian restaurant in the area and of course

she didn't pay .

My weekly order at this time had gently crept up and before I knew it I was getting 12 bars a week laid on at a high price for the time of 450 a bar which is a weekly credit bill of 5,400 . This was a huge amount and I was under pressure for the first time purely because of the vast bill I had to pay in weekly , for example if two people were struggling to get their money in to me on time and that two people had two bars each then that's 2000 down already and because the weed was tied up in debts then that would leave me trying to find the rest . Now I only made 75 per bar so even the profit off all the rest wouldn't cover what I had been let down with . To compensate for this I had my good customers who sold vast amounts in small deals and never let me down to fall back on , the likes of Clarky and Matty , they doubled their money every week and were only too happy to help if I wanted paying upfront for their next Sunday drop to give my other sellers who had fallen behind an extra week to sort their cash out and get busy for me .

 This as you could imagine turned into a daily fulltime occupation and a very hard pressured one as the people you were doing it for never gave you a minutes peace with constant calls to see how you were getting on and their rules were simple 1 - do what the boss says when he says or get a visit and 2 - never turn your phone off or not answer it and keep a spare . People think drug dealing is easy money but its not , constant pressure and fear of violence or the law , you need eyes in your arse .

 My daily routine would consist of ;

Wake up early at 7

Get up washed

Text every customer I had the same txt with offers

Respond to the texts that come back

Go to mate fletts , sit in his room on phone for two hours

Go out and about collecting small amounts off Clarky etc

Meet Sian for lunch at her request , my

expense

Get bus to town and meet other customers

Call off Archie "how much ya got in min"

Stupidly respond "should have 3000"

Tea time and once again Sian needs feeding

Pay for dinner

Get Sian to run me about early evening

Between 9 and 10 try to get my 3000

Go pay Archie

Then home with Sian for 11

Repeated the following day .

  This was tense times now as I was selling far too much , got way above my head far too soon and wasn't making near enough with the amounts I was getting to cover the usual 25 % of cash that was slow to come in which is why I used the next weeks cash to cover and eventually have to order more the next week and increase my bill again . Plus I had the added responsibility of keeping a high maintenance highly demanding girlfriend happy .

CHAPTER THREE

 I was starting to struggle with the
thousands that I had to raise weekly and
was aware that I couldn't let the gangsters
I worked for know this . To them they were
amazed with the amount that I was selling
and ordering because I was eclipsing
anyone that had done it for them before
and what they couldn't see was my
struggle because I was good at hiding it .
They thought I was great for a young kid as
my money was always in , they weren't
arsed how I got it though .
  At this time Archie was facing possible
prison after a late night police chase in his
car where he got caught with a bar after
speeding away from cops and dumping
the drugs in a garden only for a resident

two days later to find it , hand it in to police

and have Archie collared by a fingerprint match .

Archie came across all cool and handy in a fight but this worried him , he had previous depression problems , his hair was slowly falling out and was rapidly turning grey , he was thirty year old , though he had to meet the boss daily and pay him in as he was really the unnecessary middleman , which was stressful enough without his impending court case to deal with aswell .

He was expected to get 18 months and do nine for good behaviour as he was advised by his brief . This created a problem for the boss , Archie had a huge weekly order off me alone let alone anyone else he sold to and the boss wasn't giving that up so easily . Archie infuriated me by telling his bosses that I was ok to take over from him when he got sent down and put his cut in the bank for him , and in doing so set it in stone with these very unreasonable gangsters that that's what's going to happen .

Archie called me in his usual stoned dulcet tones

"Aalrite min , listen eh , nothing tae worry aboot min but the boss wants a word ken , he needs to spik tae ye aboot me gaan awa "

" Archie I'm nae so keen on this like "

He would persuading butt in

" Da worry min it'll be cool he just wants tae talk you through it min and see your set up and that "

" Aye ok Archie fit time the night like "

" Ten at yours , you can pay in then as well min "

That was that , tonight I was going to meet the illustrious boss for the first time . The boss who's picture I had etched on my brain after all the scary and wonderful stories I had heard off Archie and others , in my head he was six and a half foot tall and an evil nasty fucker , but I always thought there had to be a person under that who would obviously be charmed by my witty cocky swagger and the obvious fact of the cash I had already made this bloke . How

wrong was I to be . In every way ,
appearance , size and personality wise .

Ten o ' clock sprung upon me and I
waited home for my buzzer to go . Then
with a menacing buzz buzz buuuzzzzzz was
the nightmare I awaited .

Ever since my childhood and after many
times of tut tuts and ticking offs I have had
a tendency to grin widely in nervous
situations for which my dad always told me
would one day get me in trouble .

I let the door off the latch and sat down
ready to shout coolly
" Its open come in "
While I grinned nervously .

I could hear a thunder of footsteps roaring
up the hall stairs down the corridor and
getting louder and louder as they
approached my door . The door flung
open and in stepped a six foot brick
shithouse pierced ginger bloke wearing a
grubby vest and eighties stonewash skin
tights and boots.

I grinned .
He nodded "fit like min "

I replied " nae bad "

Following the ginger big dude came another big bloke but aged , nervous and looked like a whiz head , grey and eyes everywhere , jaws chomping up and down , looking for some respect because he was in the boss' band . He really lived in fear of the boss .

Archie followed , white as a new white sheet washed with daz ultra whites on a 100 degree wash .

" Fit like Archie " I tried to ease the pressure .

Then thumping in to squeeze into my front room came the boss ducking under my six and a half foot tall door frame to reveal the beast of a man , bigger and wider than I ever imagined and seven hundred times uglier . Growling and sneering down at me he growled out

" Fit the fuck are you laughing at , sit doon "

The smirk wiped I responded with

" Sorry err boss err Franko nervous giggle "

" Aye you should be nervous , dya ken who

I am ? "
" Oh and by the way , my car fits more
people than this dump "
  Followed by an ass licking giggle off the
ugly mob .
  Everyone sat down , no introductions , I
knew what I needed to , Archie , big ginge
, auld whizzheed , the boss , that's who
they were to me from now on .The boss
opened dialogue to tell me about Archie's
situation and that I wouldn't have to do
much different but pass on the four bars a
week that Archie sells and pay some one
different .
 " Take note min , fucking pay attention ,
this is serious shit min "
He sneered as I smirked
" We are gonna hae a trial run this Sunday
"

  His master plan was to have a trial run
with me doing what they have to do on a
Sunday further up the dealing ladder . It
gets a hell of a lot more precise and
organised as to what I was used to as
mainly a lone trader with only nervous

Archie to answer to .

 We were to plan for Archie's impending absence with me as a very important figure in how this operation ran for the morning . This was to be done on a Sunday as this is when it is always done , Sunday early morn when the world is bright but asleep , when the streets are quiet and the local working police force is slashed in half for the traditional day of rest . I was to find out that this was the opposite for the lawbreakers of the era as they knew it was safer to get more done .

 I was forewarned by 'the boss' that I would be called very early on Sunday to make sure I am up and mobile , and that they could hear the foghorns of the fishing boats and the oh so familiar squawks of the seagulls in the harbour on my doorstep .

 From there I was to go to a girls flat in Seaton near the beach to get the parcel that had two minutes before and two minutes before on purpose been left for me . I was instructed to open the package , count check and report it back with this girl as my witness , I was also told that this girl is their best punter and is clued up , trustworthy and held in high regard , oh , and that she had a skin head and took nae shit . Then from that moment on instructions would be made over the phone so I wasn't aware of any places I was to be going in advance .

The actual phone calls started on Saturday night with the boss stamping his authority on me ,

" You hame min ?" get your heed doon and am gonnae call again the morn at 7 min , and you better be up and aboot ken "

Once again he was to speak out of his backside as came 6.20 am the following day I was to be rudely awoken by the polyphonic sound of bittersweet symphony by the verve on my mobile with the name 'boss' on my caller ID.

"Fucking hell , he's keen " I muttered to myself before answering .

" Get up min , ye need to be oot o your hoose in half an hour min "

" Aye I ken min , my alarm was set for ten mins time "

And that was the most annoying thing , one thing that really bubbles my blood is when your deep in sleep , no worries and dreaming away when you are awoken rudely , you think ' oh that's ok its still dark ' before you drop your head on the pillow in eager readiness of getting back to your nectar kip , when just as you are drifting to your nectarness , a loud BEEP BEEP BEEP BEEP goes off in your lughole and you ' fuck sake ' to yourself as you realise it really is time to get up .

Any way I was instructed to get ready and get up to a phone box on the skinhead girls street where I was to wait until watching for a red fiesta to pull up , a bloke to go in and out in two mins and that was then my cue to go and get the goods .

I waited for the fiesta to shoot off in the direction of the A90 before I approached the flat .

The girl whose flat it was , was as serious as the boss , I thought I could break her down

with a cheeky smile but no chance , she
was a total misery with an icy frown and
little manners . The phone went again
.
" You got the shit min ? "
" Aye , I'm just away tae open it now "
" Do it and count em min "
" 5 k boss , 20 bars , what am I doing now
then ? "
This was the very first time I became aware
of my importance to this ugly firm , for this
was the moment I realised that these guys
now heavily relied on my work load even
with Archie in the picture . This is because
of their weekly order being 20 bars and out
of that amount , over half of it was my
order for the week . I had 12 bars and the
rest was to be dished out around the town .
I sold more in nine bars than the rest of the
sellers did in ounces.
  The boss was now being a wee bit
respectful but more authoritative when he
delivered my instructions .
" Go sort yours oot , pass your ones on that
are on order min , stash the rest and I will

bell you in an hour , right ? "

After that hectic hour sorting my own stuff out the boss called again with simpler instructions now , as if I had his trust now , not fully but there were a few chinks in his armour . I was to drop a further four bars to one of Archie's mates , Scotty in bucks burn who was meeting me at a bus stop where I was to walk with him for a hundred yards and do the hand over involving four bars , a carrier bag and a prompt ' fit like and a see you later min ' .

The skinhead girl had already had her one bar , so this just left three unaccounted for , which later on the nervous auld whiz head picked them up off me , and I also found out his name , it was Colin , fearsome eh !

That was that then , the day was the most scary , stressful and paranoid day I had in a long long time . THe boss and his heavies now knew along with me more scarily that I was very much needed by this gang as there were a lot more dealers out there now and at a cheaper price if you looked further a field .

This situation really worried me now , gave me endless nights tossing and turning as I couldn't see a way out now because of my importance . It all started a year before to get me and my mates a bit of cash on the side and a free toke in the process . I didn't delve deep enough to account for the boss , the bosses boss and so on , and how underworld and lawless morally this scene was to be for me . To cap an old cliché of the teenage mind , 'it was a laugh for cash ' .

CHAPTER FOUR

Life was very much flying by me and my youth was diminishing faster than a mega big Mac meal gone large on an American's lap.
I didn't get to see my mates too much unless it was to sort them a smoke , my true friends that I had grown up with , I had to stop my first love , which was always

football , watching the dons home and away , and playing the beautiful game . My new unfavoured past time was ultra time consuming and by now, a right pain in the arse .

I probably had two real best mates who I still saw regularly in the spare hour or two I managed to earn myself . Scotty G and Fletty . Fletty more so because he did odd runs for me and would knock a bit out , he's a clever lad but with as much motivation as droopy the dogs great granddad . He woke daily at 6pm and spent the evening in bed , quite content with himself if he had a block of sputnik ten fags and a packet of blue rizla, his mum still washed his stuff and made his tea so he had it pretty damn cushy for an unemployed uni drop out . He's cool though , I call him Monty because he reminds me in both looks and mannerisms of Montgomery burns from 'the Simpson's' .

When I had to drive out to my home village daily by morning I would always start the day at fletts , there was never a need

for ringing his doorbell as it would be a bigger surprise if he got up and answered than it would be to win the lottery without actually having a go as I don't play the lottery , I would let myself in via the back door and head upstairs to Monty's sleeping den where he had a spare bed I would jump on while mimicking Monty burns to wake him up ,
much to no avail. No sound, spillage or shaking would wake him, the only thing that did was the burning smell of a spliff wafting in and out of his ski jump shaped nose.

I would sit up there for up to two hours setting up sales and arranging to collect debts owed while I was in town . Some days I would have no sales set up or no debts to collect but knew by 7pm that I would have to head back to the city and pay in my expected daily amount of between 1500 and 3000 . Obviously very worrying to me as I lay in Monty's spare bunk bed , mobile and texting thumb at the ready .

Awaiting any possible news from the likes of Clarky who I knew would be out and about doing his best for me as he always did . I knew if I harked on at him long enough that he would absorb some of my pressure and would at least get me a third of my daily target . All this time still getting the odd call from Archie with his now annoying pointless daily question of
" How you getting on min? ".

Pointless because I would never ever know how much that I would be paying in by evening as I had nothing due by morning , I could never tell him this though or he would go into a blind panic , reduce his follicles and turn them that little bit greyer .

Fletty was never Mr popular but then I would drift in and out of popularity , but I didn't care , he would and stay at home because of it and shy away from the nutters I had to deal with . He was a really good mate though and had always been at my side and loyal to me . Some people didn't like him just because of the way he looked , we used to say his shadow came round every corner before him in a theatrical jack the ripper style . When I knew my cash was to be a couple of hundred quid down he would take in the payment for me to save me a bollocking as even in today's mad world you still don't shoot the messenger , in fact he would often ask to do it so that he could get a smoke as the going rate I would pay him was thirty quid's worth of weed and his return bus ticket . It was a two way street with us , we both knew that it was good to help each other and I was never shy at giving him a night out or few pints at my expense , and likewise .

   Sian was by now a bit of a nuisance with her demands and constant fucking about and tarty behaviour , I never had much time for her by now any way and after she made the sun newspaper centrefold one Saturday we split up , it went to her head , she thought she was famous when in reality it was a piss take and she looked ridiculous .

   I was gutted just because the fact she was

a stunner and my mates were often envious and if I am honest it was more her than me that ended it which is something I wasn't used to . I was normally the one that got bored of current girlfriends .

I gave flett a call later on from my flat in the city and begged him to come out with me to cheer myself up .

" Come oot Fletty , I'll pay your bus and get your beers min "

To which he replied in his half conscious state .

" I cannae be arsed min , im tired "

" How the hell can you be tired , you have just got up , come on min , we can go oot to the fantasy bar and I will buy you a few dances off the strippers "

" Aye ok , done , I'll get the next bus to yours "

" Nah min meet me at Slains castle boozer on Belmont st , I need a sesh now "

" Ok min bide there for us "

It was on that very night out that I was to meet the next woman in my life , this time she wasn't to be just a little girl like Sian .

She was a dancer at the fantasy bar , and as I sat at my table getting drunk and paying for Flett to have dances I noticed this cute little blonde in a bikini clocking me and giving me a cheeky smile around the straw dangling in her vodka and coke . I was a bit nervous as to ask her for a dance as at this stage of life I was a bit wary of the experience and lifestyle of these girls but she seemed different to the others and as we were getting up to go back to mine for a toke she approached me and asked for my number , I was like the cat that got the double whipped Cornish cream as Flett tutted in the familiar manner to me as if to say 'how do you do it ' . I obliged the lady's request and punched my number into her phone .

Two a.m. came along and that polyphonic sound of 'the verve ' rang out on my mobile as I reached over and slowly answered just to seem that little bit cooler .
" he'llo "
" fit like Santos , its Jenny , listen take doon this address we are goin tae a party in torry

will you come meet me , all the girls are goin "

 I was thinking , jackpot , a party of pissed up strippers with the only male company there to be me and Fletty , though Fletty was a bit scared I think and declined the best offer he has had . I on the other hand in my stoned excitement and a grin wider than cheech on the beach . I headed outside to contemplate whether to fire up the F reg fiesta that I swapped for a nine bar in the hope of one day soon passing my driving test . Contemplation lasted a mere 10 seconds while I opened the door jumped in and fired up the fiesta . I drove off slowly remembering my mirror , signal , manoeuvre for the long mile ahead , I arrived safely and full of confidence feeling like a smooth Michael Schumacher who had really just crawled along the straight dual carriage way at 20 mph for half a mile . Jenny was impressed that I had a car as she lived fifty miles away in the blue toon of Peterhead . I liked her straight away because there was no bullshit

with her , she was a wild one with a liking
for the vicier side of life , she was 5 years
older than me , we became the regular
stereotypical drug dealer and stripper and
were to enjoy many a wild night and party
at my harbour side flat . She had a kind
heart as well and a mothering nature as
she had two little ones herself . Due to my
flat being in the harbour which sounds posh
but is far far from it as this is the red light
district in old Aberdeen full of crack pushing
pimps and pissed up Siberian sailors ,
offering cheap beef and vodka for their
wages from the ships bosses . This was the
second roughest place in Aberdeen next
to Logie (we will get to that later) .
  My flat was on Theatre Lane , an old
under building cobbled tunnel led to my
front
solid oak panelled chubb secured door ,
along the cobbled tunnel you would
usually find the crack hookers used
condoms littering my path , and see them
in action on their knees just down from my
front door .

One night a freezing cold north sea chilled evening in the middle of an icy grey Aberdonian January myself and Jenny were turning the corner in the early hours to head down the cobbled tunnel when there at my door stood a hooker who was familiar to the tunnel , an old scraggly scrawny toothless crack whore who looked 49 but was really 36 and a pointless waste of a life , it was too late for her to sort her ways but with her was a very young teenager for whom I had not seen before working the tunnel , pretty 15 year old run away shivering on the doorstep . Jenny must of seen something of a younger self in this girl and she , without hesitation felt sympathy for this young girl standing on a bitter blizzard of an evening and ask them in to get warm . Jen could probably figure out that no man is going to brave this evening and forty quid for a five minute ' try to get up ' in the tunnel . And they could see this too and eager to get inside they obliged .

Once inside the warmth and comfort of

my bedroom I talked with the hookers while Jen made them bacon butties , the old one was as rough as a bears arse and laced with needle marks and bruises all over the sapping skin of her skeletal frame , she was a mess and drooling about the 12 rocks of crack she just found on a dealers mantelpiece which to her made it cool to thieve because as she kept persuading her cleverer 15 year old mate ' we found 'em ken , just lying there left on his mantel piece ' .

Beyond help , I thought . Though the young one was a worry , just new to crack after being introduced just that week on running away by the old hooker . Jen tried to get her to agree to come and meet her the next day so that she could take her up to the fantasy bar and get her some legal work with less worry and an inkling more safety . She did but shortly after we lost touch .

You see Jen was a good one at heart and great fun to be around and due to her living so far away this made me drive more on my own and basically teach myself the ways of the road though an illegal driver I regarded myself as a good one due to my experience of farm life as a youngster .

This was all great news to Archie and the boss as I had no excuse to get where they wanted me now they all knew I drove and Archie even sold me his car , nice of him eh , it was an old Vauxhall cavalier sri 140 , a mega powerful death-trap of a car especially for an over confident young new driver but I loved the power and quickly fell in love with the whole
advantages to being behind the wheel of a nice fast car . The first day that I got the car I went up to Peterhead to pick Jen up and while bombing down the dual carriageway heading into Aberdeen I managed to miss my turn off. In my inexperience I sharply turned at high speed and lost the back end spinning off road and up the embankment taking out two bollards along the way, just imagine if there was a wall there, how things could have been so different for the pair of us. I kept

hold of the fiesta as this was the perfect little granny car to pick my Sunday drop up in , a nice safe little car to slip in and out of traffic unnoticed and out of sight of the local pc dibble . All this time my stress levels had gone up and my pressure to raise cash was greatly increased as the cash I had to cover or hide grew at an astounding rate.

CHAPTER FIVE

Sat at Fletts on a fine early spring crispy morning , a beautiful day with the near frozen dew lifting off the green and colourful garden plants and the many birds singing in the red sunshine as they nip past for their feed off the ever faithful Mrs Flett …animal lover . I had the sickening feeling of not being able to enjoy the fruits of living in such a pretty place , the fear that it would all leave me and the frustration that I could never just say to myself ,

 " fuck it Santos , take today off , don't think about anything and enjoy your pals and our surroundings , go to the pub , smoke weed in the park and have a kick about , chat up some girls , do what you want , the fuck you want " .

 I could never do that though unless I

didn't care about the consequences of tomorrow , instead I picked up the phone and attempted to retrieve funds off a new customer , an accountant for whom I knew

for years and so took the chance to trust
him on three bars .
RING RING , RING RING
BEEEEP
" Hello , your through to Paul Barrow sorry I
can't come to the phone right now iam
otherwise occupied "
" Fat twat " I thought as I hung up .
  Must be at work , I will try him later .
Try Clarky , he will sort us out .
RING RING , RING RING ,
" fit like min , here don't expect miracles
from me today ken , my wee bros been
had over and I have nothing to work with
now till you get me some more , I have
given you all I can this week , there's just
one more guy I can push ken , " He said in
his usual super fast non stop speech .
" Alright Clarky , just do your best eh min ,
I am really struggling the day , Barrows let
us doon for 3 bars , put me right in the shit
min "
" Nae bother min , you know me Santos ,
and I always do my best "he replied.
 I knew that was true at least as the Clarky

would now be ultra eager to be my number 1 and keen to stand out by pulling me out the shit , big ask though , today was bad so far , really bad , it was now approaching mid afternoon and I had nothing but my petrol money to pay in .

If I am being honest sometimes just to get my cash up in quick time I would offer people I knew had cash , bars for cheap , I would text them 1 day offers like 350 cash today , offer lasting till 5 pm . Even though I paid 400 , I was that under pressure to have all my cash paid in that if that was the amount I was short then I could sell a bar for cash cheap because then I would be up to date for that week but then be already behind for the upcoming week . My logic was always that to do this was ok because I could make it back on another bar . It never happened like that though as you can imagine if this had been going on a few weeks where I would fall a bar behind a week then therefore have to order another for the next week and then after a month I am 4 bars down in cash

and having to order an extra four bars .
This was inevitably going to be found out if
it carried on or at worst if a weed drought
came where I could not supply for a week
but still had to pay in then I would truly be
in the shit deeper than ever as my losses
would be found out . I Had no choice but
to carry on and use the best advice I could
offer myself of ' cross that bridge when you
come to it Santos .

It was rapidly approaching paying in time
and I had nothing but a grand to pay in ,
this may sound like iam glamorising myself
by saying I have only a grand , believe me
I know now the value of a grand to most
people and what they could do with it , but
to me I didn't look at what could be done
with it and realise its true value , I just
looked at it and said "shit , shit , shit " to
myself as this was a quarter of what I was
supposed to get in .

Panic was quickly setting in as my phone
was blaring out the verve and flashing the
singular word ' Archie ' .

I paused while I tried in vain to think of

something to say to him , but there was nothing but the truth which came out . The boss was constantly calling him to see how much I would have to pay him and Archie was casually telling him that everything was under control , that to trust me , I never let them down and telling him that I would have at least 3 grand when in reality it wasn't, that amount would have displeased the boss let alone handing in the 1 grand that I did have , that would infuriate the big bargain bucket muncher .

Archie was seriously stressed when I told him what I did have and started to shake fully rant at me .

" Santos min , you are gona have to come with me and explain " he said .

I replied

" no Archie please , he'll go mad with me , try to put him off and I will get a cash sale or two to sort it oot min , please Archie bear with me , I have been let doon bad min "

" Ok min , I'll put him off , tell him that you are waiting on some debts but Santos min , you gotta get at least another 1500 " he said .

I was stuck , that horrible panic feeling was crawling from my toes moving up through my stomach making me feel a deep sinking like you have just heard the worst news in your life , as the panic past through my blistered texting fingers and up deep into the back of my mind creating a dark blank void in my head where my ideas and pressure responses usually come from .

This was it I thought , this Is the night my real losses and dealing methods get found out and I am for it , how will I ever get out of this .

I sat there in a car park in banchory all alone and trying as I always did to find a way out in my mind , I was truly stuck as I sat there texting like mad and having to do what I couldn't afford to do , just to save myself from the inevitable kick in that was bound to follow , I had to offer the few bars that I did have at a stupid price of a hundred pound a bar loss just to bump up my money .

Matty responded to my nuisance texts and ordered a bar for cash as soon as I got into Aberdeen . I couldn't go back yet though as Clarky may pull through for me or the twat who got me in this shit in the first place that fat accountant Mr Paul Barrow might respond to my threatening
texts of a higher force buying his debt off me . To no avail though from the tubby number cruncher . Positivity as ever from the Clarky though as he could afford to pay me an extra four hundred early , much to his pleasure and my gratitude .

I now had seventeen hundred and still eight hundred off the amount that will get me a bollocking instead of a facial rearrangement .

Shortly after as I started to drive up to Clarky's house I received a chilling call from Archie .

" Santos , the boss is going mad min , he wants you to stop whatever your doing and get into toon now , he wants you to explain fit the fucks going on "
I responded

" Another half an hour please min , I am waiting on a casher , then I will head straight to you "

I hung up and proceeded to brick it even more as I carelessly drove to Clarky's , then my phone rang again , bonus though for me this time as it was another customer taking up my all too kind offer , I now had at least half my money two thousand . I had drained all my resources bar a few outside chances of more punters taking up my offer just to save me from a hiding .

My phone was ringing again , this time the name I now hated seeing flashing in nokia green , Archie .

" Santos get into toon now , he wants to see you , what you got now ? "

I replied

" just the two now min definitely , maybe more "

He butt in ,

" never mind maybe more , just get back , he's going ape with me , he thinks you have lost control , meet me first we can go together , and I am gonna throw in seven

hundred that I have to bump it up that
should save one of us fae a doing min "
" Nice one Archie , don't you worry
though , I'll explain and smooth it for us min
" .
" Just head in now min , meet me in twenty
five mins at KFC on great northern rd , ken it
? "
" Aye , see you soon Archie "
  I surely couldn't ask for more time but I
knew fine that there was no chance of me
making it to him in that time as I still had to
pop past Mattys to sell him that cheap bar ,
this was vital as I had already told Archie
that I had this in my hand . Matty was
good for it though and himself along with
another student in town , a skater called
will were all too keen to take me up on my
incredible offer on a number of occasions
and by know the pair always had a spare
grand or so due to them getting stupidly
rich for students solely off the back of my
cheap deals when the chips were down ,
so to speak .
  As I approached Aberdeen my phone

rang again just before arriving at Matty's mum's house , shit , Archie again .

" Where are you now min ? The boss is oot in the jag with a car load looking to meet us some where min , hes calling me all the time , get here now min " he worryingly exclaimed .

I replied
" Ten minutes min at kfc , honest im just past garthdee min "
Archie cut in
" Santos he's waiting for us in a car park behind Chalmers bakery , meet us there , expect the worst ."

I stepped on it , flew up matt's stairs grabbed the cash and launched myself downstairs and out into the car to shoot now to what I was dreading and had never had to face before , the boss raging with me and tooled up with a carload .

I still , in my head was a bit fantasised and it all didn't seem quite real , that the last year had been a phase and will stop soon and life will return to normal , foolishly unawares of the dangerous depths I was delving . I drove there thinking what's the worst that can happen as I always have a dangerous thinking of finding a positive in the absolute worst of situations , I was thinking that in an hour I should be home in bed , a bit bruised but they cant murder me , could they ? Naah , for a number of reasons , they need me and I owe them thousands . So I advised my self to seem cool content , composed and fearless as I was clever enough to realise that this is the way to react around vicious bullying thugs . I raced through the dismal Granite City my heart was pumping so fast that I could hear it above the broken exhaust roar of the car .

 I got to the meet , I thought to myself , great ants , you got here before them . Things must be looking up as I searched my head for a positive . Wrong . My phone rang again as I moved away from my car and oft to the direction of the nearby dual carriageway on great northern road .
 It was Archie again as I answered
 " I'm here min , on the dueller by Chalmers

"

" We see you , we are heading round the roundabout now to pick you up"
He replied in a perky but still slow tone .
 I was now in utter fear of whatever fate awaited me , the fear magnified by the word " we " that Archie just mentioned , we , they must have got him in the car with the boss .
I stood there in the icy blast of the Granite City and did some practical sums in my head . ' a five seater jaguar , one for the boss , one for Archie , one for me , that left two spare for any hired thugs , that's not too bad , just the three . I could always outrun them if I feared for my life . Unless they chuck me in the boot and then there's room for an extra thug , I'm fucked and locked in a boot , a nice big comfy boot , there I go again with the positives , I really need to get out of that habit , I thought as I feared the worst as the jag screeched to a halt beside me and the back door flung open .
 " Get the fuck in the car " came the

terrifying voice from the driver's seat .

   Out jumped that auld whiz head Colin purposefully as so that my seat was to be sandwiched in the middle and in eye line of the jags rear view mirror where I could see the boss's anger piercing my eyes with his as he sped off to who knows where .

   I was pressed firmly between the auld whiz head and the other ginger heavy as we drove away from Logie and off along great northern road in the direction of Bucksburn . The fearful journey was eerily silent as no words were exchanged , just those baggy brown eyes looming out of the mirror towards me , which was plenty to keep me as scared as I had to be but to me the worrying thing was the fear on Archie's face . I thought either he's a big birds blouse or knows the true extent these thugs would go to . I preferred for that short moment to think he was the former , a big bird's blouse .

   The jaguar was now heading away from the safety I felt from the street lights , I now had the same feeling I had as an 8 year old when being told to be home before the street lights came on but being caught out a mile away on your own with no bike . That fear of danger that only dawns in the darkness .

The car slowed as it indicated left into a forestry commission car park where we came to a halt tucked away in the secluded car parks corner . Thoughts now arose of my family , I was far from dead or even hurt but I suppose I finally realised the disappointment and hurt I would cause to my dad , his wife , my brother and nephews , not for the situation I was in but for how they would feel for me being in that situation . Disappointment , sadness and fear for me and those close by to me in Scotland . At that time though that didn't matter to my family , I was on my own as my dad and his wife thought I was doing well at college , and my brother , while he knew I dabbled in the dodgy , he didn't ever realise quite how deep in the proverbial I was delving .

Still nobody spoke , Archie looked at me

as if to say
" You cunt , thanks "
 I shrugged and silently mouthed the words
' cool , cool ' . The ginger one got out of
the car and proceeded to the boot where
he popped it open and withdrew a blue
shiny aluminium baseball bat . I heard the
boss's leather seats creek and the car tilt
and rock as the boss turned to finally face
me and glare down as I waited for him to
talk so that I could hastily respond with a
quick thinking on my feet answer that I
prayed he would want to hear .
" Well " came the question .
" Well what boss " I daftly replied .
" Why you cheeky little fucker , where's my
fucking money gone ? "
 He shouted down at me .
" Err eh , sorry boss , its nae my fault " I
replied only to be cut short .
" Hang on a fucking minute Santos , you
had the shit , you pay for the fucking stuff
ken , now what the fucks going on , right
now min you are saying fuck all I want tae
hear , I want fucking answers min .

" Aye Boss it's under control , I have been let doon bad min for two grand " I replied

  He seemed to drop his shoulders a bit and be a little bit more insightful as to what I was saying .

" Santos min , if you have been had over then we have debt collectors who can buy it off ya , all we need is the name and address min " He enquired .

" No please all I need is a couple of days to sort it , I can come up with enough daily to pay it off to you before the next load needs paying for min boss " .

  Still I continued to help and cover for the same fuck ups that had put me in this position , though the boss now listened to me as I seemed to come up with a solution he was just about content enough with to let me leave with all limbs and facial features intact on the promise of utter misery and pain if I didn't stick to my side of the bargain . To be honest , there was only one side of the bargain to be kept , my side .

  What worried me now was the fact that

the boss was telling me that he was cutting my order until I had steadied my ship , and he capped my load to three kilos of sputnik . I had always needed the relief easer of knowing that I had more nine bars to call upon if I needed a quick cash sale to top up my paying in money .

  The main thing now though was that I was walking away , and like I said before , I would be in my bed In an hours time and safe for now from my feared outcome

Chapter Six

People I wrongly associated with around me were now a lot calmer and eased off me a bit in anticipation of the short wait I had promised I needed to get everything under control .

That next day my phone was going crazy for the previous day's offers , but there lied the problem , I was desperate last night and to save my own neck I would have even sold my bars at half price that previous night . That day though I wasn't as desperate and had a day longer than the few hours I had previously had . This confused my regular customers who were puzzled to why the exact same stuff was now fifty quid a bar dearer than the day before . They thought I was pulling a fast one on them individually and probably felt singled out by me to fork out the latter price , they would never believe me if I told them that they got it cheaper than I did therefore making me a loss in my desperation to cover other peoples fuck ups and piss takes . So I offered them the same deal but with a slight altercation on the hope that they then wouldn't be able to take up my kind offer .

 I thought that by offering them the same price for the one bar but on my one condition that they had to buy four to get the deal I offered . I thought in my under estimation that that amount for cash upfront was just out of their reach regardless of how deep I had made their pockets in the past year .

Can you guess what happened ? Depending on how you look at it the either clever or stereotypically miserly Aberdonians could not tear themselves away from the long term saving that they could be making , and I did grossly under estimate them as after all they were mostly educated men from the private universities of the town . They went for it to pull out all the stops and unbelievably rally round and work there three day worn socks off to secure this bargain for themselves while I still prayed that four individuals would singularly come up with only enough for the dearer price when buying just the one bar each . Out of the ten people that received my offer thankfully only the two took it up , which was good for the short term and a big boss pleaser for a Monday nights pay in .

I couldn't bear to think about the near future and would always scramble my sane thoughts that would flood the back of my brain , scramble those thoughts of the utter diabolically stupid , scary and

unbelievable situation that I was in . Block
them out with the only line of thought I
knew , the line I carelessly lived by of ' cross
that bridge when I come to it , something
will crop up ' , all the time
knowing that something most likely wont
crop up and I could be in for a gruesome
climax one day .
   To get back to the current situation on
what was Monday paying in time , and the
eight bars that I had sold to the two people
gave me a good £1000 over my usual
amount which impressed the boss and
had Archie nearly choking on his Prozac
when he phoned for his daily update of '
how you getting on min ? ' .
   This was good and bad for me , good
because at that time I only ever thought
the one day ahead , I blocked out any
terrifying thought or calculations as to
where I stood financially if there was to be
no more weed and I wouldn't be able to
sell it or I just stopped , the latter being
theoretical as to just stop would be suicidal
I was led to believe by the fearsome

bullying big lump of lard of a boss . This , I
was told would incur a buy out fee of
around 50,000 pounds .
  I know what you are
thinking........ridiculous.......stupid.......unbeli
evable......impossible , why not just fuck it
all off and do a runner ? Most of you will be
thinking , but the consequences to me
were terrifying , I was just a kid , which is no
excuse but I knew I had got into a hole , or
a deep deep pit , I had family locally
including babies who would be targeted if I
was to leave without a trace . I was
frustrated that I couldn't let go and tell
some one , to seek out advice or help but I
wasn't like that , I saw my problems as my
own and I knew that it was half
embarrassment and half the fact , that it
was only my problem that I let nobody
know what was really going on . In all my
life I have never been one to ask for help , I
would tirelessly seek out solutions for my
own problems and many a time would
successfully turn around many bad
situations while knowing deep down that if

the very worst came to the worst in any form in my life that the one security that I had , that I always had throughout the years was my father , he raised me and battled for his kids throughout our early years and taught us the best and showed us the best in all we did while he never really said it , but we knew he loved us to death no matter what we did , he always knew and knows that there is good in us . After all , he is a good man and he must think to himself that we have his best qualities inherited in our genes .

I now for the first time realised that I was in serious danger of my debts doubling in the weeks to come as I sold too much to the wrong people for the wrong price . I knew that I now definitely had to look ahead or I was going to get hurt and my family would be in danger .

The fact dawned on me that my father would have to find out about what I had been up to for years , there was no easy way to tell him and absolutely no shortcut to the story , he had to know , and he had to know the whole truth . I risked losing him but hoped and prayed that as he had so many times previously , he would have a solution because I couldn't for the life of me see a way out . I realised that then was the time to tell him as the haunting image in my head of the alternative was for him to find out when it was too late , when it would be the police knocking on his leafy Hampshire cottage to inform him of my untimely death at the hands of evil bullies , and that my body had been found in a ditch by the a90 motorway and that he had to identify me . This was always a real image in my head as I tossed and turned , legs wrapped round the duvet at night in an uncomfortable state of non sleep .

   The following day I was up early as ever due to my recent state of insomnia and was summoning up the confidence to call him , but I couldn't do it , I chickened out and did a terrible thing , I text him instead . I can't begin to imagine the horror , anger and disappointment he must have felt as he opened the text and read it to himself .

It took about five minutes for the call to come back to me , at first he was angry but this calmed as he felt my despair and like any parent , they feel there children's pain more than the child themselves , an instinct takes over for them that they want to somehow transfer that pain onto themselves which just isn't possible sometimes , but in this case it could be . We could both see a way out , a financial way out that was possible but I daren't ask , instead I waited for the question to come to me ,

" so ants , how much do you think it will take for you to buy out of this , get your debts in some sort of order and start again with a normal life ants hmm? " he said sombrely resigned to the fact that he was my only help while desperate to do so .

I was still embarrassed then with the major mistakes I had made and stupidly at that point made an underestimation . Now with all the people that let me down before for payment and the debts I had incurred that I was cleverly covering with cash sales , I was probably down by 8,000 all in all to start again .

I figured though that if I had an instant injection of about 4,000 then I could work tirelessly for a week , maybe pull off one last scam or run , to clear myself , so that's what I did , I told my father that 4,000 would be enough to clear me of this evil mess that was dragging me down and eventually would drag others around me with it . I really did need to work hard with that sum , I was too embarrassed to ask for more , it admitted blatant stupidity , and the slim chance of proudness being sought from my father would be out the door for good , I felt that four grand was a ridiculous amount of money to ask for , I
daren't ask for double that figure . I couldn't foresee the snowball effect when you are constantly chasing money , because while you do this your debts worsen and soon you are back at square one while along the way having exhausted the only real help that I did have .

There was also another option to me

which I shied away from more for other people sakes than my own . You see when my debts were beginning to be found out by the bosses firm they tried to drag out of me who owed me what as I was informed by the ugly mob that they had an even uglier mob of smack head debt collectors who would get these debts in by any means necessary in exchange for some cash and a bit of the brown stuff . All they requested from me was names and addresses and they would take a 25% cut of the debts on collection . Thinking back now I am still in two minds whether I should have done this , after all these were the debtors who had got me in this mess in the early months of my selling that forced me into bigger loads just to try and cover them . Like I said before , the snowball effect .

My father called me back shortly after and filled me with an enormous feeling of saviour and relief , before we spoke I was hanging around back streets of Aberdeen , ducking and diving around , not wanting to sit at home , fearful of the boss threatening my inactivity and with this I felt like I had the weight of the boss on my shoulders , and the boss was a beast of a man . My dads offer of help felt like a ladder being put up and the boss on my shoulders cheerfully climbing down . I felt good again and enjoyed the next hour or two while I awaited a bank transfer .

I could finally see a way out of this mess , and soon , have my life back and enjoy my youth as I had already wasted a toddler's generation chasing cash.

CHAPTER SEVEN

   Shortly after the funds from my dad
landed in my brother's bank account I
gave Archie a call .
" fit like 'en Archie , I've some good news
for ya , my old man has given me a sub to
help us out of all this , give it a week or two
and I will be squared up and ready to
leave it all behind and sort you whatever I
owe you once Franko's paid off "
" Aye really ? Fucking magic min , that's
made my day ken , I was panicky aboot it
all " he responded .
  It was then I started to think about how
the boss would take this , I thought at worst
that I may have to go away for a while but
then I could come back to my home and
hold my head up debt free and free of any
harsh illegal ties .
  I have never been more wrong , after all ,

I wasn't dealing with a fair minded

generous businessman , no , I was dealing
with the boss , a big ugly beast , torturer of
bag heads and bully to the weak , a bloke
who profited from the fear he falsely
injected in his terrified mates/addicts/sellers
.

  What was I thinking , he wasn't just going
to let me walk away from this , no , I really
did have to just pay him off and leave town
. That's what my father urged me to do ,
wise advice , but I loved Aberdeen and
that area , it was my home , my town , my
kinda people .
  I then asked Archie to not say any thing
and just work together to clear this mess up
before it got way way more out of hand .
  I was too late , Archie had slipped up in
an earlier call to the boss where Archie
mentioned to him that I wanted to clear up
and stop . Whoops , I can now imagine the
boss on the other end of the phone with
steam hooting out of his ears and his
face going beetroot red in a cartoon style .
t could imagine him pointlessly angry , and I
say pointlessly because I wasn't now a

roaring success for him , I was a liability , cracks had appeared long ago . A half decent businessman could of figured that out and would of took the wise approach to cease trading with me now that he made his money and there was no more to be made .   The boss wasn't a half decent business man though , in the past he had profited from bullying antics thrust upon terrified addicts .

 Instead the boss sneakily pushed more weed on to Archie who in turn thrust it onto me , I was weak , and they both knew I still needed to make a lot more . Archie knew exactly how much and himself urged me to take more as he himself was tired of all this and wanted to go back to the days where he sold just the 2 bars , 1 to his mate and one in ounces , he wanted out too while the boss was just slightly suspicious and a bit naïve to think that violence could some how magic up some cash that simply wasn't there . He wanted to keep me in debt to him so as not to lose my customers , and probably because he got rushes for the power that he felt he had over people .

When Sundays paying in day came along a few days later , I was pleased enough with myself and confident for the first time in a month or two of getting my money in on time or at least the most of it , give or take a grand or two . This was good for me as usually I had only half the money by Saturday night and was always ran off my feet and physically and mentally drained trying to push my total up .

Archie usually helped me to do this by sneaking me an extra bar or two on tick for the week and half the time , due to his fear of the boss , he would put his profit in , hopeful that I would be able to square him up soon after .

I collected my new load which I was eager to make the last and at the same time gave Archie what I had to pay in which he added to his and our overall total to me was a pleasing 9000 out of the debt for the week of 10000 .

I didn't fear any repercussions from this because I had paid in a lot less in the past without concern , after all the boss made a meaty profit from his vast prices that were thrown upon you , rising with inflation as if his boss wasn't some shifty Irish/Glaswegian knife merchant but Gordon brown , the then British budgeter . I knew the boss must of nearly doubled his money as I knew of places where I could get it for nearly half the price although I was forewarned that if I was to do this then I would end up wrapped in chicken wire and bricks and slung into the north sea off the back of a shaky fishing trawler .

I was now relaxed at home on my bed with my glasses on and smoking a Columbian woodbine while reading that months loaded magazine when my phone flashed the name Clarky ,

" Fit like Santos min , how's it gaan ? " He said

" Nae bad Clarky , I did well the day so I'm having a chill at hame for a change , fit can I do for ya " I answered and questioned .

" Is it cool to send Steve in tae grab us a

bar min , im all oot and I can pay ye 3 ton the now ken " He asked .

" Aye , nae bother Clarky , send him in on the 201 bus at 8.15 , I'll dig it oot for ya " I replied .

" Cool cool min , I'll speak tae you in an hour or two min when stevos safely on the bus min " .

We said our goodbyes and I carried on my leisurely activity as I was enjoying the part weightlessness of my shoulders and the relaxed feeling I had which to me was a rare glimpse of the feelings I had as a part concerned unemployed 16 year kipping in my girlfriends mums pub , always then seeing a way up and forward as I was beginning to see now .

Then suddenly and startlingly I jumped as I heard a THUD , THUD , BANG BANG , THUD THUD , BANG BANG on my chub secured solid oak front and only door .

My first thoughts were , ' shit it the feds man , im getting a bust ' .

I made sure there was no traces of chopping weed in my kitchen and I limbered towards the front door , as I turned the latch , SLAM BANG , the door was forced against the hallway wall with me squashed behind it was slammed open and those familiar thumping of feet marched through my hall into my bedroom , all the time the boss ducking under every door frame .

I was pushed along the corridor back to what 3 minutes earlier was my chilling out place , I was pushed back onto my bed , I still had my glasses on . I surveyed the situation and head counted and was anxious as to what was going to happen to me and why it needed five big bastards to do it .

The boss sat on my armchair on the left of my bed followed the next biggest bastard , the ginger one , in his stonewash denim and white vest sat on the right side of my bed . The other three stood at the foot of my bed , upright against the wall , looking and acting like a bunch of ugly violent dogs ready to be let off the leash for a dog fight , and I was the opponent.

The boss leant into me as I sat in the middle of my bed , glaring deep into my eyes , so much so that my frown began to match his .

 " Why the fuck are you sat at hame , reading a fucking magazine and supping tea when you still owe me the day , eh " He quizzed aggressively .

" Franko min , I haven't stopped all day , I've nearly squared you up , and I'm due some payments in the morn , I'll have more than what's owe to you " I answered nervously .
And with that he leant into me again still glaring at me through my reading glasses , he slowly lifted both hands to my face , I flinched as he removed my glasses . I knew what was coming as he said
" Wrong fucking answer " and nodded at the other animals who pounced on my as I was centred in the middle of the pack , I curled up as a flurry of punches and kicks came thrashing towards me . I threw my arms around my head to protect my best

bits and good looks and took the punishment soundless as not to show a weakness .

" Enough " the master declared to his masturbators , and the pack withdrew back to there original leashed positions .
 Then bang bang on my door again , dazed , I pondered who this could be , the police , more heavies , or Steve . I was slung over to the window to have a look , it was Steve .

" It's a punter min " I turned and said to the boss .

" Aye , good " he said
He pushed me along the corridor with the ginger one in tow , they hid behind the door as I answered it .

" Go Steve , just go , get out of here " I shouted , but the boss reached over me and one handed grabbed Steve by the neck and drew him into the corridor pinning him against the wall with a crash .

" How much fucking cash do you owe Santos " he screamed at steve .

" He owes me fuck all , he's a good punter

, my best " I interrupted .
" Really , good , sorry min , go on fuck off
and dinnae breathe a word to nae fucker ,
ken " the boss said as I nodded approval
to Steve .
 I was then flung threw the corridor again
and back to my room where the boss
followed his assault on steve with the
commencement of one on me and he
throttled me against my bedroom wall
planting my head against the wall with a
thumping sovereign laden punch to my
nose , a stream of blood covered my white
shirt and sprayed the flat walls as the boss
held me up to stop me sinking to my knees
as he turned and said to me ,
" Did that fucking hurt " .
 I was dazed I though it was a trick
question , for example if I were to respond
with the words ,
" Yes boss "
I thought he would probably turn to me
and say as he planted another nose punch
" Nae half as much as that min "
 I was half unconscious and didn't know

what was happening .

" didnae hurt boss " I stupidly declared .

 " you fucking what min , didnae fucking
hurt eh , you cheeky little shite " he spat
angrily at me as he raised his fist again
straight armed and threw another 24 stone
into my now gushing face .

 Once again as I sunk to my knees the boss
then dropped his arms to catch me as I fell
and propped me back up against the wall
to once again repeat his earlier question .

" Did that fucking hurt min ? " he sneered
down at me again .

  I was just regaining the consciousness t
had just lost twice in the space of five
minutes , but I made damn sure that I
responded with the answer that he wanted
to hear ,

" aye boss that fucking hurt " I said flinching
in preparation for another punch , but the
punch didn't come and I looked into his
eyes and I may have been dazed ,
confused or whatever but I swear I saw
regret in his eyes as he carried me past my
blood splattered white walls and into the

bath where he took my white shirt off my back and began bagging up the blood stained clothing and sealing the bag as if he had just committed a murder , the man was a paranoid wreck , I thought , so why push stupid situations like this .

I changed and cleaned my self up as the rest of the ugly mob removed personal items from my bedroom , like my passport and emergency contact and next of kin details .

I now couldn't leave the country and the boss had acquired my personal information which included my mother and fathers separate addresses in England . That was as good as collecting the debt to them , as they smirked on leaving .

" See you the morn Santos , and you better nae be late min , ken " I was chillingly warned as they slammed the door behind them .

Shortly after the ugly mob had left , I jumped up as I heard a key in the door which to my relief was Barnes , one of mates from banchory and now flatmate .

He worked for my elder brother as a chef in one of his golf club restaurant franchises .

Now barnsy was a bit nervous and a very shy boy , he preferred to spend his days off and nighttimes by sitting in front of his play station and listening to his favoured Indy music or bands that I had introduced him to from my native Manchester , he shied away from female attention and stuck to the clothes that he still found fashionable from his early school days like chord trousers , dodgy shirts and his chequered chef pants , I could never let him know about the depths of shit that I had got myself into as he would have run a mile .

As he entered the flat I could hear him mouthing his ' fucking hell , what the fuck has gone on here' as he shouted my name and with a slightly slow muted response I would answer back , ' in ma room Barnes '

.

He walked in quizzing and stunned as to what had gone on , I had no choice but to tell him as there was blood still on the walls and he could see my room was no longer in the usual tidy shape that it was .

  I never wanted to tell him as he was close
to my brother Jay for whom that he worked
for and would undoubtedly feel that in
telling Jay , he felt that he was doing the
right thing , I on the other hand didn't want
to worry Jay , as he was a worrier , he
wasn't like me in that sense , to me when
things were bad , I always thought 'fuck it ,
ants , there's always a way out ' , but Jay
seen things how they were, to him a
problem was a serious problem .

  And with that I told barnsey the full story
and shit that I was really in on the promise
that he wouldn't let our Jay know , he
reluctantly agreed as I promised him that it
was all nearly sorted .

  I cant hold anything against barnsey for I
had put us all in this position and with that
he promptly packed and jumped back on
the 201 bus to stay safely in his mums back
bedroom , protected from the big dangers
of harbour Side life living With me

  Surprisingly for me that night I slept really
well , most likely due to the fact that two

hours before I had been beaten to the point of unconsciousness .

  I awoke the following day to that annoying ring tone of mine that I now dread ringing every time the fucker went off , I looked down to my bloodstained bedside table , briefly remembering the events' of the night before for which you always tend to forget that first brilliant 19 seconds of the day , and the name Jay was flashing up on my illuminated screen .
'Barnes man ' I thought
 He's told our kid , I don't want this .

CHAPTER 8

Now Jay knew I was no angel as he himself bought what I had sold , but he didn't know how much trouble I was in , I was good at hiding it , I had become an expert in that field .

I tried to convince him that it was a one off but he wasn't daft , he knew better , he himself had been in similar trouble in the years previous but had knuckled down and was going through a golden patch in his life and in that previous week had just had his second son with his fiancé .

He backed off when I told him that I would get it under control , he even went to the bank that morning and arranged a surprise loan of 800 pounds for me which I had to turn down , partly because I didn't want him getting his family into debt for me and partly because 800 pounds didn't really touch the sides .

Archie was the next caller with his daily question of ' how you getting on min ? '

I told him not to worry that I would have the extra grand in for tea time .

I thought that would be that for the day but come 3 or 4 pm that day , he called again and asked where I was in the town , I was dubious as to know why he wanted to know this .

He said to wait on chapel st where he was going to come and get me , the boss wanted me round at his flat and not to worry , he just wants a chat .

He picked me up in his white cavalier sri and drove me to the boss's flat in the council blocks of great northern road .

The blocks were made up of four two bedroom flats , we buzzed and were promptly buzzed in and Archie led me up the stairs to the top right flat , we heard the unlocking of the solid door started with a chain noise at the top moving slightly lower to a bolt above the main lock , then the main lock where the noises proceeded down to two bolts at the bottom .

For a second I thought we were going to see the crown jewels appear .On entering

the flat it was fort Knox , it was only a two
bed council flat for gods sake , and
already I would hear the mechanical
movements of cameras and could see four
doors off the corridor in front of me and all
of them were guarded by a pin number
entry system that I was informed the boss
only knew the numbers to it .
  The boss was towering in the corridor
glaring down at me when he turned and
said
" ma next door neighbour is a mate and
he's paid off , he wont hear you scream ,
the auld dear doonstairs is deafer than an
earless mute and the other flat is
unoccupied , so nobody will hear you , ken
"

 And hear was me thinking there was
nothing to worry about in coming here , I
was now scared , specially after the events
of the night before , I was petrified , I didn't
understand , I looked to Archie who
shrugged , what the hell is goin on , I was
utterly confused .
  The boss gripped hold of my shoulder and

led me to have a look out the kitchen window .

" see that blue van min , that's for you " he calmly pronounced

" me boss , why ? " I nervously replied

" see that man putting shit in the back of it ?"

"Aye"

" That's for you he's putting in bin bags and shovels "

Then it dawned on me , was this the day that I had dread for all the time I had been in this mess ? Was this the day I died ? Was this it ? , I was scared , really scared when he dragged Archie and I into his bedroom to line up as if in a firing line against his bedroom wall , as I looked around his bedroom it revealed all the hall marks of a psychopath , a big massive television screen with 6 separate screens built in revealing all that was goin on in every room of his flat . Paranoid freak , I thought .

This fearful idiot had loads of children but not one picture of them anywhere in his flat , instead on every wall of his bedroom he

had photographic portraits of his dead dog done up like it was on a modelling shoot for 'pets r us' , with pretty ribbons on its head and flowery bowties round the dogs neck , deranged , I thought again .
What the hell was now going on .
 I could hear the thumping of feet marching upstairs , I knew it was the rest of the oh so familiar ugly mob , I was getting used to that sound by now and with that came the knock on the door and fort knox was opened up again to allow them entry . They entered the bedroom , the ginger one and some one I hadn't seen before , a small stocky built lad with cropped blonde hair and small evil little eyes , eyes that with no facial expression expresses anger .
It turns out he used to be an army PT instructor and now he's a hired thug , there was now four of them guarding me including the boss .
 I was up against the wall and the Biffa the blonde was stood snarling through his nose to my right , he was bouncing and rattling

on his toes when the boss nodded him he unleashed a fast striking punch to my opposite eye , fast and professional with a clenching of the fist at the point of contact . It was so quick that it was a sharp blow to me with little pain so I flinched slightly and maintained my position , head still where the dog picture once was .

There was an eerie silence as the boss looked to his watch and with that , one of the phones that sprawled his bed began to ring in its unfashionable old style two ring tone . The ugly mob looked to the boss before looking to each other .

" Fit like min ." The boss answered .

A pause followed as who ever was on the other end of the line spoke before the boss responded

" aye min , we got him , he was halfway to Dundee when we caught him , he didnae hae the twenty five grand though eh " .

I looked to Archie and for a brief second thought that they were talking of some other lad until my brain started ticking over with thoughts of what was really happening

.

' Twenty five grand ' I thought , what was happening because I certainly didn't owe them twenty five grand .

It was then I realised that not only was I a bit down on my cash but that they also were a bit down on their cash and they dealt on a much larger scale than I did so a bit down to them would have been thousands maybe into the tens . The guy on the other end of the phone was the bosses boss and the boss was informing him that I had lost twenty five grand of their money .

" Take the phone Santos he wants you " the boss puffed .

" Hello " I answered .

" When was you born Santos , eh ? " I was quizzed in a scrubby broken Glaswegian accent spoke like a true Glaswegian in a high toned voice as if he was speaking out of one side of his mouth .

" December 1978 min , why " I asked .

" Santos Stewart , born December 1978 , Died April 2001 " Came the chilling response in my ear as my shoulders dropped in a resigned swoop and my thoughts fell south out of my head leaving only the one thought left , the one I had dreaded for over a year , dead , the end , conclusion to it all . My life flashed before me , my dad smiling at me , my dad being proud of me after a game of football , my dad shouting at me , my dad frowning in disappointment at me and the worst one of all was the face of my father I had never seen before except in my nightly nightmares , the face of an adoring father who had just lost one of his sons that he raised divorced from the mother . Total sadness .

I now knew that tonight was the night I would most probably die and there was very little that I could do about this as I was taking the fall for this lot , I may have been able to turn this around if it was just the bosses mob that I could talk round but now I believed that they were following the orders for the hit on me .

I had to think , think hard and think quick .

I needed to summon up some options in my head and do this with in 30 seconds .

Right , I thought , option 1 - I figured if talking out of it wasn't a likely option then I could run out of it , I knew I would have to pick my moment and that I had the 1 chance to run away and not face certain death in a horrible way . I thought that they wouldn't be able to tie me up until they got me to the van as we had to walk out the block of flats , past some other blocks and cross the car park to the far corner where the van was tucked away out of sight of most buildings . So , I looked around the room and confidently thought , yeah , I can do this . The only other person in the room who may be able to catch me would be the army guy , though he was late thirties and not at his peak of fitness that he would of once been and if I were to use the element of surprise then with a quick burst of pace I could be able to get a fifty yard head start in my pursuit of the safety of the brightly lit dual carriage way of great northern road .

Option 2 was an after thought that promptly got under way when the boss declared ,

" right min , you ready ?"

" please boss , dinnae do this min , there's always a solution " I responded .

" Nah Santos min , there's nae this time , that's it game over , my bosses call it a result , if the cash aint recovered then a body must be the result , that's the way it is , its over " . He explained .

" Would it nae be better to recover the cash then , then every bodies happy , you ken , please " . I begged .

" How the fuck Santos , eh , could you get us 20,000 , you ken cos that's what we need ? " He responded .

I then went on to say some thing I regret but it saved my life .

" I can raise ten by tomorrow night and I will ask my dad for ten the following day , please , give us a chance min . " I said .

" Maybe you could get ten for the morns night but how the hell do I know your auld man is gonna cough up eh ? " . the boss replied .

" My dads minted , I know he will do it for me , please , trust me . "

" Right , I fucking will , but you listen to me min and fucking listen hard . "

" I will , anything " relieved , I responded .

" Shut up and fucking listen hard Santos , you pay us the ten you owe us and then we will call the other ten grand , a buffer , dya ken what a buffer is min ? " Asked the boss .

" Aye , its what a train bounces off min . "

" We call it that cause you will pay for your usual order and then match it with a buffer which I will look after for you until you steady the ship . " . He said .

  Now I was thinking.....Aye , whatever , like they would ever give me it back .

" When three months is up then min and everything is in order then I will gie you it back in full , ken " He continued .

 Relieved of at least of a way out of this flat alive tonight that I would of agreed to any terms to walk away , death still loomed for me after all that very night and even though I knew I could at a push get ten grand together then I thought I might not be able to ask my dad again and could try talk my way out of the other ten grand as it wasn't a debt any way that I owed to any one bar probably Archie who had chipped in for me now and again to bump up my paying in total .

" I'm happy with that boss , at least I know its there to back me up any time " I replied but only in a sense of sucking up and trying to act like I was fooled by the bosses sudden brain wave when I just wanted to get out of that flat as soon as humanly possible with everybody happy .

" Right then min , the morns night at 8 pm say , you get to me the first ten , aye ? , you reckon you can dae that Santos ? " He pressed .

" Aye , course I can , I'll push some regulars , sell a few cashers and call in some favours " . I answered .

I was thinking of getting Clarky to push for a grand out of his regulars and like wise with a few others while I could also offer my cash paying custom a cheaper second order if paid for upfront , anything , I thought just to leave this flat now and spend the night in my own bed , warm and safe apart from the odd prostitute tapping on my window for a lighter for which I had learnt to avoid however persistent a cracked up sex slave was .

" Word of warning though Santos , we will be on your backs all-day , I will send some of my lads to your brothers work and anywhere else I know of , we will fuck your family up if you snitch , do a runner or dinnae pay up , ken , you fucking hearing this Santos ? " He warned in a stern tone .

" Aye boss , I wont let you doon , I'll sort it , thanks for the chance to prove it min , I appreciate it "   And strangely I did even though it was only half my mess and I was dragged into a whole lot of other shit through this lot , I did appreciate it because I no longer felt that I was going to die tonight which I really did feel half an hour before .

My emotions had swung from fear , hurt ,

scared , content , pleased to finally elation
that Archie and I would be driving away
from here tonight .

CHAPTER 9

 As I lay in thought on my bed that evening
I realised that it was coming to a
conclusion one way or another and soon ,
maybe one week maybe two but certainly
with in the month . It was going to end in
one of three ways. Either I pay in and
knowing the boss wouldn't want to lose his
best customer then I would have to leave
town with my head held high knowing that
I didn't owe him anything and absolutely
delighted to finally be out of this whole
mess after two years of stress , struggling
and run down illness due to this horrible
trade that I had mustered up for myself .
  One of the other ways would be for the
grim reaper to finally catch up with me
after all the struggle and the shit hit the fan

again and like a cat I would be on my tenth life , the after life .
  The other would be for me to get caught

by the police and to earn a way out by doing a stretch of porridge at her majesties pleasure , which sounded attractive though I don't know if I could handle not having female company on a daily basis apart from the old dragons of screws that would pound up and down the wings in the ancient slammer of HMP Craiginches.
  I knew a climax was approaching as I walked endlessly through the back streets of the granite city racking my brains for a solution.
  It was now seriously time to get it together and get busy, busier than good old Richard Branson and that bloke is busier than a Chinese crèche, he runs hundreds of businesses, has a family and children all while trying to get from one end of the world to the other in hot air balloons or sailing boats .
  I had to crack on, make calls, send texts,

offer offers. I had to raise the buffer plus the extra ten grand to pay for my load and that's a heck of a lot of dosh to fling together in the one to two days I had to get it. I still didn't want to ask my dad and as I walked around Aberdeen city centre responding to texts and setting up cash sales for the evening I sharply realised that that evening could be a de ja vu scenario all over again as most of the people I needed to raise the funds from were obviously workers apart from good old Clarky who had never ever had a job in his life. This meant that come four or five o'clock I would be horsing around all over Aberdeen and Deeside to make collections leaving me no time for alternative measures if one deal fell through and if two deals fell through then I really would be up the tree without a ladder.

I had to keep pushing as the day went on making sure that I could get ten people to go for the grand each deal that I had put on the table, all were keen and things were looking really good for getting in my desired amount.

The first person I needed to get his arse moving was Clarky , he was slowing down and seemed to be out a lot with people I never knew, people from the city who were all from the muggier scruffier side of the coin. This left him less time to be the eager beaver he once was for me, his motivation had vanished in the space of a couple of weeks

When I got out to the village there was no sign of Clarky or his mate Stevie, no phone on and not at his mums, even mini Clarky didn't know where the hell he was. This was out of the ordinary for Clarky as he thrived on being my Mr important though that was now not much to be proud of.

While out in the village I had managed to gather a couple of thousand so far from a few students who were available for a meet.

I wasn't too concerned about Clarky not pulling through for me as he always turned up with the goods on time or early and he knew I needed a grand from him that day so I had put that down in my book as a banker. That would of gave me enough so far to be a third of the way to what I needed that day with a couple of hours left before the workers started to meet me and do some business.

I managed to get hold of Clarky's mate Stevie and he was just as much in the dark as I was to Clarky's whereabouts and he confirmed my fears that he had been hanging around the shiftiest areas of Aberdeen amongst the bag and crack heads. This worried me because of his eagerness to please people and he didn't have the sharpest of minds and so I feared for him being taken advantage of. Stevie said that Clarky went to town last night and was half way to being wasted then, god knows what the lad will be like a day later if he was still going strong on the lash.

Stevie had a couple of hundred of his money to throw in the pot and I collected another grand out in the village before I had to make my way back to town to catch the workers who were finishing and the odd university student who were eager for my deals.

Archie continued to call with the famous line of 'how you getting on min?'. I was pleased with the progress that I was making and told him so but I knew only too well how things could change in an instant in this game and so I kept busy on the phone and texts to bump up my total.

I was now only four grand away and had 6000 in my hand, it was now 6pm and in the words of the great Sir Alex Ferguson ' squeaky bum time ' .

I had a definite extra two thousand to collect before eight pm and five maybes along with the possibility of Mr Clark turning up I figured even if half of that didn't happen then I was still bang in line to reach my target of ten grand for the day,

I set off to see a student who lived in the shadows of Pittodrie the home of my beloved Aberdeen football club, he and his flatmates bought from me regularly to supplement their income and I had tempted them into a deal worth another grand. Students being as meticulous as they are were on the ball and paid upfront in full to creep my total up to just over two thirds,

I was getting a lot less nervous and growing in confidence of an early evening free of violence and any aggro.

Still no word on Clarky but I was ok with this, as I have said before, Clarky always paid and always showed up in various states of stupor.

The next stop on my evening was an older bloke called kev who used to buy ounces for cash but recently has been tempted to up his order, he was due to pay me £500 and he became my first let

down of the evening as he was still miles from home working as a driver heading back from England.

Still, I didn't worry too much but I was slightly aggrieved as I had wasted half an hour in spinning round to his flat near mount hooley in my Renault 5 gt turbo.

A couple of my 'maybes' then let me

down for between four and six hundred pounds while another student on my next stop in Sunny bank handed over seven hundred and fifty pounds leaving me just 2250 to collect but I was starting to get pressured to crack on and things were drying out and still no grand from Clarky, I now had to discount him from my total and move on to collecting a few two and three hundreds that I had indebted to me around the city centre,

It was now eight pm and I had eight thousand pounds and was really getting stuck for ideas and running out of time.

I had news from a mate in Banchory who had just finished work late and just received my texts on charging his phone, it was a bonus as it was another thousand pounds but it was an hour round trip and that meant getting back to town at nine pm earliest and leaving no time to get anymore. I jumped in the old turbo and flew to the village along the south Deeside road zipping round corners like I was perfectly safe with in a fairground go-kart. I grabbed the grand and zipped back to town thinking that I could go and see if kev's back yet and that would be that and even if kev wasn't there I still had ninety percent of my total and was sure that the boss would be sound with this although he couldn't see the work that had gone into my day to push that total up and the stress that came along with, head exploding stress.

All he wanted to see was ten thousand, the ten thousand I had promised to get the night before, the ten thousand that I offered in fear of my life and others.

AS I stood ringing kev's buzzer my phone began to ring again and once more flash with terror the word 'boss', I looked at the time on that flashing screen, it read 9.15pm I was fifteen minutes late.

" Times up min get to me now I'm at Charlie's in Logie, nae fucking aboot min just get here in ten, ken" The boss barked.

" Nae bother min" I replied.

Kev wasn't in yet so I had to boot it up great northern road in the turbo to get up to logie in the fifteen minutes that I was allocated .

On Archie's instructions I pulled up in a car park around the corner from Charlie's to meet Archie and go together in his car. He seemed shaky on arrival and a bit concerned with being a grand down as I tried to convince him it would be fine as I had never had such a good paying in day.

I was a bit nervous too and was full of mixed feelings because on one hand I had started early that morning with no cash to hand and thirteen hours later had pockets full of used notes totalling nine thousand, surely he would be quietly impressed as the boss must have been thinking the worst with my recent slow record. I considered this and thought that the nine grand must please the big man.

We stood on Charlie's doorstep awaiting an answer, Colin answered and ushered us in to the back bedroom of his council bungalow.

" You better hae some fucking good news for me the day " harked the boss.

" I have had a good day boss I've been busy a' day boss, from this morn….." I was abruptly interrupted mid sentence.

" Shut the fuck up min just tell us what you got and it better fuckin'' '''''''' start with a one and end in four zeros " Shouted the boss.

" Boss I did well I got nine grand in I can get the extra one tomorrow cos a mates on his way back from England with it for me ken " I confidently declared.

" nae good enough min " He said.

There was a pause though when I first told him my total, a five second pause where I could swear I saw him accidentally nod approval. He must have been pleased, surely it helped him and me out of this mess. The boss still insisted on stamping his authority on me and not just stamping it on my toes, he was stamping it on my head with a pair of size twelve doc martins and over twenty stone of Aberdonian.

" I am gonnae do you a favour Santos, I am gonnae give you another hour to save your life min, now get back oot there in your motor and get me my grand" He so kindly offered.

"Right I'll see what I can do but I'm stumped boss there's just one lad I can push " I sighed.

" Well get oot there and push him, get back here for half ten with my fucking grand ".

My emotions flipped from fed up sighs to frustration at being bullied to pure frustrated anger at what he was hopelessly making me do at an almost impossible time of night to gather any real success. Was this a test, was it just to prove his power to me or to the other meatheads surrounding him at the time.

I jumped in the turbo not knowing where the hell to start and I sped off into the country and out on to the narrow winding south Deeside road with my foot to the floor. I didn't care at this point if I lost control on a corner and plummeted down the steep banks into the frozen river Dee. In my mind I didn't want to give that power tripper the chance to do me in and would rather do it myself to piss him off big time.

After driving frantically for ten minutes along the country road I reached Culter on the outskirts of Aberdeen and pulled up without realising in the car park to my old football pitch from when I captained Glendale Gliders under 12's ten years before. How I wished that moment for the turbo to be some kind of magical mystery time machine and transport me back to that innocent time when I collected my two player of the year trophies on that very pitch on the closing day of the 1990-1991 season.

Back to reality and I had to clear my mind and think. I did something I had never done before in front of my closest friends, I showed a weakness and text them all to let them know how much trouble I was in that evening and asked to loan small sums from each of them.

I then realised that I wasn't alone in that country, I did have true friends who cared as the response was unbelievable as a flood of texts came back to me. A few people could loan me £100 each, one lad said he would give me £300 and I called in a debt of £200 while one of my best childhood friends said I could keep or sell his pride and joy brand new play station 2 which I sold to my other flatmate Scotty. I had done it, I mean we had done it. It had took me an extra 15 minutes on top of my allocated hour but I had the grand that he craved to get his power fix. It would take me another fifteen minutes to get it to the boss which I told him as he rang to speed me up.

 I arrived at Charlie's house at just before 11pm 'bag of sand' in hand.
" You definitely got my G min? You fucking better " The boss boringly pressed.
" Aye, here, its all there " I replied and handed him the wad.
" See min, you can do it with a push in the right direction, that's all you need min " He smugly declared.

  The boss was chuffed to bits with himself and there is a lot of bits that make up that man.

I should have been pleased too but I had given him kudos and reason to believe that I was a money machine and with more pushes in the future I guess he figured that I could repeat same procedure for the big man as and when requested which was just one more headache to me to go with all those other lead weights on my worn down sloping shoulders.

  With that I made my way to the front door only to hear the disastrously terrifying reminder ,

" Same time, same amount the morn min "

Echoed in broad Aberdonian down Charlie's hallway.

CHAPTER TEN

I awoke the following day with various of
the big mans warnings echoing around my
now thoughtless mind. I was still 50 - 50
whether the situation was settled due to
the previous days 'pay in', on my part it
really was wishful thinking and just a small
hope that I was now clinging onto with my
worn out trembling fingertips. A hope that
they would see the torture, stress and pain
that they had thrust upon me and a hope
that they would realise they had already
won and should wisely walk away with
cash in hand and a tortured victim for the
ugly mob to pride about some where in a
distant background.
 Hope vanished with a startling D D D DER
DER D D D, D D D DER DER D D D 'one text

received ' appeared against the backdrop of flourescent green light on my battered over used mobile phone.

I opened the text and the senders name read BOSS, and the message was just as terrifying.
It read - 'Get to fucking work', now this might not sound very scary but in my head I could see the picture of a seven foot monster weighing more than giant haystacks and big daddy put together spitting those four words down at me.
" No fucking about today min, I want that ten, I am nae in a good mood, early, dinner ken? " continued the big man.
I felt that empty sinking feeling again, I was worn out, it was morning and somehow the boss wanted me to repeat the unthinkable of the day before. Well he thought I would get it because as I told him earlier if worse came to worst then I could ask my distant father who had proved a valuable life line before but I knew that

amount was ridiculous for me to ask him for and to transfer it same day, no chance.

I rose and washed and walked up the cobbled hill from the harbour and down through Castlegate into the town centre. The day seemed unusually bright and there was a crisp but pleasantly warm feel to the air around the usually bleak, grey granite dull features of the often wet and dark city.

I on the other hand knew the directions I was taking on foot but didn't know the destination, I was a man/boy lost in his home town. My head was spinning and trying to bypass the conclusions that I knew I would have to come to.

I continued to walk up through union street and took a left past the jobcentre where I stopped to ponder for a second on the steps that I had run up on many occasion previously to sign and declare I have not worked recently and was available to do so.

A couple of girls I knew past by and proceeded to examine my forehead, strange I know but I was cut bruised and rather used to it, they weren't as I made up the old excuses that I bumped into a door and managed a wry smile to let on that my comment was in fact utter shite.

Break had, I continued back to my trekking and returned back down union street, through the graveyard and stopped above the shopping centre to sit again outside the post office. I was doing all this walking and thinking so that I was out and about, in public view and this always made me feel safe. I had to sit down and think hard, think really hard as I could see a good way or a bad way out of this and either way it would be that day.

Once again my thoughts turned to my dad as I tried to put myself in his shoes, imagine how I would feel if my child was in a mess like mine, I suppose to convince or persuade myself that to call him would be the best thing to do. I concluded that if my child was in this mess then yes I would have to do all I could to sort it for them but then again that is easy for me to say not really knowing how this would feel for him.

It was like I had a halo wearing white sheeted bearded man hovering above my left shoulder and a nasty red horned little bugger hovering above my right prodding and pulling at me, I didn't know what the hell the to do so I sat there, thought fuck it, and text my father. He could wash his hands of me or help then I knew where to go from here. I thought he simply wouldn't be able to help and would have to wash his hands of me. I didn't even know where in the world he was at that time as he always flitted between London and somewhere in the former Russian state of Kazakhstan and if that was the case then there was really a faint slim chance of some guidance that I so desperately sought.

I continued to sit and think for a further five minutes when my mobile rang and flashed the name dad. I had to answer it quick but was so nervous as to how he took my plea for help and for the first time in my whole life he swore in frustration at me, he was quick to respond to my text and had no time to think, it turned out he was driving and was stunned with what was going on, my bottom lip started to drop and tears welled up in my eyes in the middle of the busy city and it was hurt towards what I was doing to my family, I was deeply hurt at what I was dragging my dad into and I could sense that he was stuck as I fully proceeded to fill him in with the whole story.

My father tried to calm my cries and assure me not to worry but I was, I was being pushed once again for another ten thousand pounds that I didn't have and didn't owe. I told him of my imminent death and the threats I was regularly receiving, the pressure I was under and how after over a year of struggle and managing to scrape through bad situations by this point though I was ready to give up and take what was inevitably coming to me. My dad ended the conversation with calming words of 'don't worry son' and 'for every problem there is a solution'.

"leave it with me ants, I will get back to you

soon" he assured me.

 I felt a wee bit better like there was a pinpoints worth of light piercing the end of a very long dark dirty tunnel.

 I stood up, wiped my eyes with my sleeve and headed down the steps and through the bon accord shopping centre and off up George Street when my phone rang again and without looking at the name on the screen I prayed for it to be dad as I answered.

"Where aboots are ye min?"

 Shit, I thought as Archie's familiar dulcet tones spoke down my ear.

 "In the toon min, why?" I replied.

"The boss wants ye min, I have to come for ye, dinnae worry just tell us where aboots ye are and I will pick you up" He calmly assured.

"I will bide here for you outside John Lewis', how long" I said.

"Five minutes min, don't move".

 I thought, oh aye, here we go again as I was resigned to the fact that I was most probably going to be terrorised, hit maybe and spat familiar words down to but knew for the sake of everyone around me and the slim hope things would be fine that I had to go and face up.

Archie pulled up in his white M registration cavalier s.r.l. and the passenger door flung open in readiness of me jumping in.

I explained to a scared looking Archie that my dad was going to sort it out but probably couldn't get a bank transfer that day as it was a Saturday. This worried him and he made me very aware of this and we carried onto great northern road in silence and off into the bordered up concrete jungle of the gruesome estate of Logie.

We pulled up outside a block of six flats that I had never been to before , three of which had sheet metal bordering the windows and doors to conceal its emptiness.

Archie buzzed one of the flats and a girls voice answered as she buzzed us up.

Still silent I followed Archie up the stairs and into a flat on the 1st floor where a small stocky lad I hadn't seen before was busy moving long thin shaped objects from a back bedroom in to a stacked pile against the wall in the corner of the living room. As he passed he politely asked if we wanted a cuppa to which we both said yes as we were led to take a seat in the front room by the girl who promptly directed us and then left the building.

To me this looked liked another psychological battle of terror and seemed so far like quite a tired one in comparison to the bosses previous efforts, I was quite calm as Archie sat biting his nails and shaking slightly.

The auld whiz head Colin arrived next to nervously take up his offer of a brew as he sat down with an eyes wide open scared look to drink his tea.

The lad who's flat it was introduced himself as Napper and then took a call on his mobile.

"I have the two rifles, a baseba' bat and a couple of pool cue butts min"

I figured that the boss was on the other line

as I was passed the phone by napper.

"Santos you seen the film 'the fly'?" The boss snarled.

"Nah min" I calmly replied.

This seemed to anger the big man.

"you've nae seen the fucking fly min?" He again pressed slower and louder.

"Nah min" bored, I responded.

"Well, there's a saying in it min, it goes 'be afraid, be very afraid', in five minutes my mate pinheed is gonna get there and do ye ken why we call him that min?" He continued to quiz.

"Nah min" I repeated.

"You seen the film hell raiser min?"

Fuck me I thought, is this Film 2001 or a tactic of terror, just get on with it.

"Nah min" I replied.

"Because he's a mad wee bastard min" he gravelled.

"And then in ten minutes fae now, I'm gonnae to get there, so be afraid min, be very afraid" the boss continued.

We continued to sit in silence, Colin on the couch opposite doing some extreme nail biting and Archie sat alongside me on the other couch also heavily involved with his own fingernails while I sat in thought. Napper was in and out preparing the obvious crime scene and the auld ginger Charlie was hovering in the corner looking out the window and down to the littered street below.

In unison we all jumped and turned our heads as the buzzer menacingly rang out in the hallway.

Pinhead was in the building and as he entered I was slightly amused as the fearful pinhead waltzed in smaller and skinnier than me and was clearly called pinhead not because he was a 'mad wee bastard' but a little smack head heroin addict. I guessed he was tagged with the name because either he stuck a lot of pins in himself injecting that nasty shit or because more logically the eyes in his little tennis ball head were constantly pinned from the abuse he did to himself. He came bouncing in though looking agitated, gasping for a hit, cigarette dangling hands

free from those scabby lips and eyes
everywhere.
"the boss is here min, you all ready?"
Charlie warned from his look out.
No buzzer as he let himself up with a key to
the block.
 I could hear those thunderous footsteps
thumping up the stairs slower than a
second count. They got louder and heavier
as he neared the flat door and swung it
open. In he came more hurried now and
without looking to any one else he made a
dart for the scared looking Colin who raised
his legs and hugged his own head in
preparation for a beating.
"You got my fucking money Colin" He spat
loudly.
"Boss I'm a grand doon min, I'll get it the
night though ken? I have been let doon"
he responded from the breathing hole in his
head hugging arms.
 The boss then stomped into the corner of
the room to the upstanding weapons,
chose the blue steel baseball bat and
swung round to Colin striking him hard on

the legs, pure anger in his red drooling face
he proceeded to pound Colin's legs and
protective arms a further five times
with the most extreme venom in his baggy
eyes.
"Now, give me your fucking money" he
snarled at Colin.
 Colin painfully and regularly flinching
rummaged in his pockets and pulled out a
bundle of used notes which they both
folded into hundreds and counted up.
 On completion of their counting it ended
up that when Colin counted up on his own
that he had actually miscounted and had
over what he was due to pay that day.
"You fucking stupid wee cunt" the boss
jibed to a sore, shaken Colin.
"Now your turn min" he turned and spoke
to me.
"Fit the fuck are you saying min aboot this
other ten grand, you got it?" he angrily
quizzed.
"Boss its nae in ma' hand but its sorted,
hear me out…"
"Nae good enough, Napper, Pinheed,

drag that wee shit in the fucking kitchen"
he ordered.
 I thought what the fuck new tactic is he
going to inspire the ugly mob with now, is
he wanting me to stick the kettle on and
make him a slice of toast at the same time
or is it more sinister and am I in for another
beating, The latter seemed more obvious
by the sight of the blades and Stanley
knifes that lined up across the worktop.
 I wasn't that bothered by now about
getting a beating, I was very used to it and
growing immune to the physical harm that I
received.
  Pinhead grabbed my right arm angrily but
weakly and thumped it down on a crumb
coated chopping board, Napper did the
same to the white stiff looking Archie.
 Pinhead and Napper grabbed for a blade
each and in typical little smack head style
they both chose the Stanley knives and
rested the shining blades on the base of our
trembling fingers.
"Those fingers dinnae seem to be working
do they eh?" asked the boss.

I stayed silent in preparation for the next move.

"They didnae manage to get my ten G yet have they min so I might as well chop them off, go boys" he said while instructing Pinhead and Napper to carry out his obvious pre-planned routine,

Pinhead with a fresh cigarette dangling hands free once again from his mouth pressed his head into mine and tried to scare me with his wasted glare. He was agitated more and I could see he was in need of a hit which wound him up even more as he proceeded to slowly drag the blade across my fingers just managing to scratch the surface.

"Now what the fucks happening with the rest of your buffer min, you said the day it would be sorted, now where is it" he pushed.

"My dad's going to get it to me but he cannae transfer it the day ken" I promised.

"Nae good enough, pinhead, napper, cut them" he ordered.

Pinhead dug the blade into my little finger

and ran it slowly along the other four cutting every one of them.

I was now scared of the next move, I didn't want to lose my fingers when this was so close to being resolved, I thought that if they did chop them off then they might show mercy and let me get to hospital with them in a bag of ice and for the first time in a couple of beatings I really did show fear and begged them to stop, promised it was sorted and rambled hurriedly to them that it would be in my brothers bank by Monday lunch time. I packed so much information into them ramblings to plead for my fingers and a true resolution.

I looked the boss in the eye and I could see emotion in those baggy brown eyes as he slanted his head towards me in thought. A pause for a second or two and then he ushered me outside to the balcony adjoining the kitchen,

We stood opposite each other backs to the railings as he pushed the door shut to gain some privacy. His shoulders sank as if to relieve the pressure of keeping up his hard man act and he looked to me sympathetically.

"You know min when this is all done you can be one of the boys again, come round and play cards with us ken, when your house is in order which I'm beginning to think it will be.."

"It will be boss, Monday" I butt in.

"Aye ok min, I am starting to believe you ken, so far you have pulled through when pressed so I think you can min," he continued.

"Just get it done min and we are all happy, chill out tomorrow, I'll call you a couple of times and then come Monday I will send Colin to the bank with you to get this done, ok min?" he said calmly.

"Thanks boss, I wont let you down, I mean it" I replied.

"Right go min and again don't tell nae fucker aboot today ken?" he urged.

"Aye ok boss" I reassured.

I left fairly unharmed and was given a lift into town by the relieved Archie who pleaded with me to end this like I said on

Monday.
I had a day and a half now till I had to face them again so I arranged to go out with a new girl I was seeing, the distance between Jen and myself had ended us and I was seeing a fit young lass from Northfield called Clare who agreed to meet me and we went out for the night and I have to say that I really enjoyed the evening with a host of gorgeous young lasses and me on a crawl around the best bars in the granite city.
Sunday was spent in bed with a hang over and the odd contact with my dad about the 'loan' he would be giving to me. So with everything set up for a bank transfer to my brothers bank in Banchory for the next day I got my head down early and slept like I was on two tubs of diazepam.
I was awoken by my alarm bright and early at 7.30am on the Monday and there was a pleasant aura to the bright and breezy harbour side as I looked out of my window.
I was energised, fresh and ready for the completion to this nightmare that I had

dreamt about for months and months.

I got dressed in my best white pressed shirt and black trousers and made my way to the bus station.

The bluebird number 201 bus was waiting engine warming for my date with destiny and a dream of being free again in the town I loved to do what I wanted when I wanted.

My first stop was my friend Flett's as I was informed the bank transfer wouldn't take place till eleven a.m. or there about and so I had two hours to kill while I waited for my brother to finish doing the breakfasts at his restaurant.

As it approached eleven a.m. the boss rang to confirm everything was fine and issue a stern warning that it better had be and just in case it wasn't he informed me of thugs awaiting me where ever I may turn if it doesn't go to plan, I was made very aware that this really was my last chance saloon. He also told me that my taxi awaited and will be waiting right outside of the bank in the form of auld Colin who would drive me safely into Logie to complete my torture and hand over the final part of my buffer.

We arrived at the bank and there was a feeling that the bank knew exactly the importance of us being there as if they had been warned although paranoia was getting to us all.

We were ushered to the managers office as a cash withdrawal of that amount could not be done over the counter as it had to be counted twice in front of me and bagged up in a yellow cotton bank bag complete with drawstrings.

I could see out of the bank managers window that Colin was indeed parked up in his Audi Quattro partaking in his favourite pastime of nail biting and flinching. I arose from my chair to leave with yellow bag in hand when my phone rang.

"You sorted then min, cash in hand eh?" quizzed the boss.

"Aye min, I'm on my way out to Colin now, we will be with you in twenty five minutes" I answered.

"Good min, it feels good, does it?" he praised.

"Aye see you soon".

I pleaded with my brother who wanted to come and guarantee my safety, nice thought but seriously the wrong thing to do as the boss would see this as an insult and probably fill him in as my brothers brave front was no match really for these violent thugs. He left on the promise I would call him when I got there.

The twenty five minute journey seemed like ten as I sat in silence while Colin rattled on about his own shit gangster activities and pure crap about him being a millionaire by the time he was fifty, and he was then forty four. I sat as giddy as a child on Christmas morning all the way till we buzzed Pinheads smack flat where we were instructed to meet.

Nerves then set in as I was entering a strange flat with a bag of fifties so fresh that they were still warm and smelt of freshly cut wood.

The boss shook my hand and the rest of

them gave me a sarcastic clap. I just
wanted to be in and out of there.
"Well done min, I knew you could do it" the
boss praised.
"You wanting a brew Santos min?" Asked
Pinhead now in a calmed relaxed
smacked up approach.
"Nah, I need to go, my bro's worried about
me." I said eager to leave.
"Ok min then just let me double check your
cash and you can go, you can still get stuff
from us, come round and play cards min
and be our mate ken? We have a laugh
do we lads?" he said to the nodding room.
"I'm just glad to be out of it min" I replied.
 The boss raised one eye away from his
counting hands but then dropped it to
continue to count.
 I left alone, declining the offer of a lift and
waltzed down the stairs with my chest
puffed out, I opened the blocks front door
and breathed in a deep breath of that
cool salty Aberdeen air and tasted its
cleanliness for the first time in a year. I then
made my way home to spend the night on

my own relaxing and getting over the torture of the previous two years. I was happier than I had ever been that the

conclusion was the best out of my earlier options, all was healthy and all was safe.
 Then my phone rang.
"I have been doing the maths and something you said to me earlier made me think Anton, you listening?" It was the boss quizzing....again.
"Aye" I huffed.
"You said you wanted out so you can do but I need to pay the lads for what I had to get them to do to you at Nappers the other night" He continued.
"Three lads at a thousand each, plus Archie says you still owe him two grand from when he bailed you oot over the last few months, sort that and you are free to roam the ton min".

CHAPTER ELEVEN

One of my customers Matty came round that night and we sat in my room sharing a conversation and pre roll spliff when my phone rang.

"F-f-f-fit l-like errr Santos min" Slurred a wasted sounding Clarky.

"Easy now Clarky, where the fuck have you been for two days min" I asked.

"I I am f-f-fuck o'd m-min" He stuttered.

The phone went dead and I was unable to get back through to him, his battery must of gone. He sounded really bad but he was a large binger and had been in worse conditions before now as witnessed previously by myself. So I left it alone and continued to enjoy an evening of my own company after Matty left.

The bosses offer or idle threat of paying him five grand I thought was nothing to worry about as to pay to get myself beaten up was a ridiculous ask. I could avoid that one and put Archie off personally as I knew plain and simple that he craved closure so would be heavily relieved to be out of this situation and would willingly wait for his money as long as it took to get back. So I went to sleep happy and with only thoughts of growing up and seeing what I could now do with my life with all the extra free time that I would now have.

The following morning I went for a walk as a free man and filled my lungs with the salty air.

I felt my mobile vibrate in my pocket silent against the backdrop of the Union Street traffic and saw the name 'dad' flash on the screen.

"hey son, how's things now?" he asked.

"Good dad but he reckons I owe him another five grand for getting beaten up the other night, I don't know whether to take it seriously or not but it is worrying me still, will it ever stop" I told dad.

"Anton give me his number let me see what we can do this is getting ridiculous and there is only so much at hand to help, I am running out of money and time in all this" he huffed sympathetically.

I had an incoming call.

"Dad I will text it to you he is trying to call me now" I ended the conversation.

"Alright Franko what's up?" I answered.

"You got that five grand yet min?" quizzed the boss.

I gave out a little chuckle in disbelief at what he again thought was a walk in the park.

"fit the fuck are you laughing at min?" he screeched.

"your having a laugh boss, is it raining money again today eh? I didn't realise" sarcastically I replied.

"Why you cheeky wee shit, where the fuck are you" he pressed angrily.

"Kill me, do what the fuck you want I have had enough of this shit, my dads gonna speak to you" I told him.

"He better fucking sort it, I still wanna
fucking see you about your fucking
cheek min, where are you?" he
urged.

"Think I'm gonna tell you so you can send
one of your arse lickers to get me to take
me somewhere for a day of torture from
smack heads desperate for a bag, no
chance, just leave me to sort it out and
wait for my old man to deal with you" I said
on hanging up to the big man.

 My brother then phoned and said he had
just spoke to dad about me and wanted
me to wait on a back street in the town
while he sped in to help me stay safe. I
waited on Holborn Terrace in a doorway
with my collar zipped around my mouth
and a white adidas baseball cap covering
my stressed head.

 A mere twenty minutes later and my
brother screeched seriously to a halt at my
side, flung the passenger door open and
urged me in, quickly.

"Dad's spoke to him, the bloke reckons that

if you we pay this last five grand then its all over and you are free to walk the streets , they said they wont even look at you if they walk by you, do you believe them" Asked Jay.

"I dunno, this has gone on and on, whats the alternative?, how can I get the cash?" I asked back.

"Dad believes him and has told him he will transfer the cash through to the bank this morning and that it should be there for two pm today" Jay assured me.

He continued.

"We need a plan if anything fails, any ideas?"

I had a think and always being a quick thinker I came up with a plan.

"Aye, right here's what we will do, they are gonna have people waiting at the bank again and keeping an eye on my flat, they don't know where you live do they?" I asked.

"Nah min, why would they" he replied.

"Good, I'll phone the boss and tell him that we have to be in the bank for two when

really we will go in at one, the bank reckons half one at the latest it will go through, ok?"
"Carry on" nodded Jay.
"I will tell them we have to go to the bank in Culter as its dads branch, that will buy us time and make us safe to go into the bank that we do actually use ten miles away" I continued.
"We can go to yours and wait to go, get some shit together and be prepared to move the kids quickly if we have to, and get Lucy here with her car as well" I ordered in case we had to go off in different directions, get the kids away from me and me away from them.
I then rang the boss and instructed him of our bluff plan all though every thing was true apart from locations and I hoped I could cross that bridge of query when i came to it.
"Your dads a clever man Santos, he talks a lot of sense and we are finishing this as businessman to businessman, I will be waiting outside the bank in Culter for ye', I wont be alone remember, just get it done"

The boss seemed happy.

"I just want an end to this, now" I pleaded.

"No probs but I want a word with you about your cheek earlier, I cant be seen to take lip like that" he demanded.

"Nah min that's it, closure, after this my phone goes off and I don't wanna cross paths with you lot again, I will pass you the dosh in the street through the car window and that's it, done" I demanded back.

"Right, your call, see you at two" he surprisingly agreed.

Jaime's wife Lucy turned up after leaving the kids safely out of the way at her mums country cottage. She hurriedly packed some of the boys things together in preparation for the worst case scenario.

I made a brew while Jay rolled a calming Columbian woodbine while we killed off an hour before our fates were to be met.

Jaime drove us to the bank and we went over and over our plans for scenario a, b and c till it was etched to our numb brains.

The bank manager greeted us pleasantly as they do if they think you have a lot of money. He walked us through every door he held open with a broad grin on his face. He sat us down and ordered his secretary to bring us a fresh pot of coffee and close the door behind her.

"I have spoken to your father and he has informed me of the importance of this transfer going through but because he is out of the country now there will be difficulties at such short notice" warned the manager.

"Yeah but it will definitely go through today though?" concerned I quizzed.

"Do not worry Mr Stewart I am ninety percent positive of the transaction being smooth" he reassured me.

It was now half past one and we stared at the bank managers computer screen which he had kindly tilted in our direction.

My phone rang out too and broke the silence. It was the boss.

"Where are you min, you haven't gone into the bank yet min, I'm here" he snarled.

"I am min, I'm in the managers office now"

" Well fit the fuck's happening min?" he

grunted.

" Its been transferred, all we are waiting for

is it to go through for two pm ok" I

responded.

"Right, will you just hurry the fuck up min,

Colin's getting on my tits" he fumed.

 The bank manager continued to tap his

desk with his biro and stare blankly at the

tilted computer screen.

 I looked up to the clock on the wall, it

read 2.04pm.

" I am so sorry Mr Stewart but it would seem

that the transaction will not be available for

withdrawal until 9 am in the morning "

sighed the manager.

My heart sank into the pit of my stomach, I

turned to Jay and mouthed the word

'fuck' with a horrified look on my pale face.

" Switch your phone off Santos, lets go. "

ordered Jay.

We ran out of the bank and straight into

the car to carry out our back up plan.

I knew by now that the ugly mob would of

gone through the bank and realised my

bluff. They would then head for my home

town of Banchory which made them hot

on our tails at a mere 15 minutes behind,

we had to swap cars yet to a car that they

didn't recognise as to lose any tail we may

have picked up from any waiting cars in lay

by's.

We got to the village of Strachan where

Lucy awaited us in her unknown car, It was

quickly decided that Lucy will take me to a

station and Jay stayed with the kids. Now

we knew that the ugly mob would have

people watching the bus stations, the train

stations and at the airport so we

took the decision to head south with

baseball caps covering our heads. Dundee

at 50 miles away was a bit close to home

so we carried on another 100 miles to

Edinburgh and deep into the heart of the

capital To Waverley station.

I just wanted to get on a train that hadn't

come from Aberdeen and head as far

south as I could and then take it from there.

A train to London was due in 5 minutes

and with a wink and a wave I boarded.

I sat down as paranoia eased, looked

around the carriage and breathed a

massive sigh of relief.

The wheels started to hiss and squeal. Was I
now free I thought, was this the end of it all
for which I had seeked out for so long, I was
yet to know for sure as the train started to
set off in its southerly direction as I sat and
pondered while staring at the beauty of
the hill top Edinburgh castle. We used to
have a saying in Banchory based on one of
Jonny Mathis' most famous songs. It goes
'that boy's Jonny Mathis' and with that I
was gone gone gone.

The End .

Clarky made his last phone call to me that

last time we spoke or I spoke and he

slurred, and I later found out that it was

most likely he died while talking to me as he

was found dead that next day.

The police intervened from there on in

following death threats to my step mother

and father which forced her to bring the

police into all this which was the last thing I

wanted.

They set the ugly mob up in a bank transfer sting which failed and forced the ugly mob underground and on the run for 6 months while they prepared their get out story for the police.

They handed themselves in confident of their bull shit story and set about there much contradicting case for defence which constantly dug them deeper and 2 years after the event they were jailed for 11 years.

Manufactured by Amazon.ca
Acheson, AB

13547475R00092